Enjoy! Karen Poirier

Karen E. Poirier

Across a Prairie Sky

A Country Gardens Book

First Edition – August 2014

ISBN
978-1-4602-3556-0 (Hardcover)
978-1-4602-3557-7 (Paperback)
978-1-4602-3558-4 (eBook)

Produced by:

FriesenPress
Suite 300 – 852 Fort Street
Victoria, BC, Canada V8W 1H8

www.friesenpress.com

Distributed to the trade by The Ingram Book Company

Table of Contents

Dedication

Long ago, when I was very young, my mother used to entertain me with stories of her childhood growing up on the prairies in Manitoba. It was a very different world than what I was used to--a magical world filled with young adventures in a rural prairie setting. Although I was certainly inspired by those stories, this book is a work of fiction, a product of my own imagination.

I would like to dedicate *Across a Prairie Sky* to my mother, Olivene Knibbs who patiently explained the many details that were important in the creation of this story. I would also like to dedicate it to my grandmother, Eleanor Kate Graham, who I am sure was watching from above as I wrote this book.

Karen Poirier

Nell

Chapter 1
A Friendship Is Born

"Eight, nine, ten, ready or not..."

"I'm coming to get you," a small voice sounded in the distance.

Ellen peeked around the corner of the barn and listened.

He'll never find me, she thought.

She twiddled with a bright yellow dandelion and began to pull off the petals, two by two.

He dropped his chubby little hands from his eyes and stepped away from the rough brick and concrete wall. His blue eyes and light hair, flattened by his hat, sparkled like gold sequins in the sunshine. He turned, hesitated, then bounced over the flower beds around to the front of the house, his feet narrowly missing the red geraniums and clipping off some petunia leaves.

As solid as a faithful friend, the little red brick two story house stood breathing, sprung from the earth, like the garden, overfull with energy and love. The windows were open to allow the breeze to filter through the white cotton curtains and give buoyancy to the little black flies buzzing in a circle. Their home was surrounded by a patchwork quilt of rolling green and golden fields, tumbling and abundant with wheat, flax, corn and grass.

Surrounding the fields were warm wooden fences, woven like a basket, containing but not isolating the farm. Above the prairies the wide cobalt sky was a playground for somersaulting puffy white clouds.

William ran past the open screened front door to the other side of the house. A wooden rain barrel sprouting a cloud of mosquitoes was a good place for her to hide. He giggled, then crept up slowly. His small hands touched the rough slivery wood and the cool metal rings as he peered around it.

His sister was nowhere to be seen.

Where did she go he thought.

"Ellie, Ellie. Where are you?"

No one answered.

He sat down in the grass, pulled out a blade and chewed on it while he thought about where she might be hiding. A clicking blue dragonfly hovered over him. Its delicate transparent wings trembled, then took flight into the warm summer air. William's cheeks were slick and pink with the summer heat; his yellow straw hat was damp against glistening hair. He wore a white cotton shirt and short pants cut off above the knees revealing reddened knees, scratched mosquito bites, and chubby, tanned and dirty legs. He ran barefoot in the cool grass and damp earth.

The barn, he thought, that's where she is.

He ran down the path behind the house, skipped over the slotted metal cattle gate to the large imposing barn, its cavity gaping and wide. The dark, cool, shadowy barn subtly lit with blue and purple shadows smelled of fresh sweet hay.

"Ellie, are you there?" he called.

He didn't really want to explore inside the barn looking for her, so he decided to search behind the barn first. As he came around the corner he saw her sitting in a crouched position, her head down and covered by her browned arms. William snuck up and poked her. Startled, she jumped up, hesitated, then ran up the hill towards the pig pen.

"No fair, Ellie. I found you. Come back. It's my turn to hide."

"Have to catch me first."

Ellen, laughing, stopped to catch her breath and leaned on the gate of the pen where the pigs lived. She didn't notice that the latch was undone, and as she rested against the wooden gate it gave way and opened. Ellen fell to the ground in her surprise. First, she heard the squeals and grunts of the over-sized pink giants, then she smelled the animal odour approaching her. Fear gripped her young body and she was only able to roll out of the way of the charging, squealing pigs as they thundered through the opened gate towards freedom. Now behind them, she saw their jelly-like rolls bounding down the path, their heads nodding up and down in approval. Ellen heard some loud snorts. Frightened, she turned and saw their two large, angry sows looking at her from the pen, their snouts black from digging in the cool earth, nostrils pulsing with agitation at the tiny black ants running down their necks and at the loss of their piglets. They exploded towards the opened gate, pounding the ground in their quest to follow the others.

"Run, Ellie, run!" called William.

On her feet and running for her life, Ellen hardly dared to look back. She could hear their grunts and feel their heavy breath as they charged behind her. Just when she thought that her life was over she felt herself being scooped up in the air and pulled out of the way. Her dad had her under his arm and with the other arm waved and shooed at the sows, stopping their charge and sending them back into the pen. He closed the gate and waited there for the others.

Ellen's breathing started to slow down when she realized that she was out of danger. Her arms wrapped tightly around her dad's neck, only loosening when the tension started to leave her. She breathed in his smell of sweat and saddle soap and she didn't want to let go, snuggling against his strong and comforting chest.

"It's okay now, Ellie. The pigs won't hurt you," he said.

She slid down and stood as close as she could get to him. In the distance she could hear a pot being banged and her mother calling,

"Here pig, pig, pig."

Her mom was carrying a metal bucket with pig feed in it, shaking it and offering it to them. Finally, the renegade pigs followed along behind her, single file, away from her precious garden. She led them up the path and back into their pen. Their reward was a manger full of fresh pig feed.

Ellen shook the dirt off of her blue-bibbed overalls. The overalls were fastened on one side with a button, and the other side was tied in a knot covering her short, puffy-sleeved gingham blouse. Her loose dark curls haloed her bright blue eyes, sunburnt nose, and freckled face. Her feet were bare and summer-toughened to grass and bites.

Coming out of the pig pen, her mom gave her a disapproving look, then turned and went back to her work hanging clean washed laundry on the clothes line strung from their back porch. The dancing white sheets and the diapers were first washed in boiling hot water outdoors, then hung up to dry.

As the sun rose to the center of the sky, the smells of dinner being cooked drifted towards them. There was no need to call anyone. Mom was making bread, that was for sure. That unforgettable, yeasty smell of bread baking in the oven along with the aromas of roasting meat, fresh corn and potatoes from her garden called their empty stomachs to the kitchen looking for their noonday meal.

Ellen came through the front door, down the hallway, and into the kitchen.

"Ellen, is your dad coming in to eat?"

"Yup, he's coming right behind me."

"And William, where's he?"

"He's with Grandpa. He went to help pile firewood."

"Better tell them both that their dinner is ready. Then go wash your hands."

"Okay, Mom."

Ellen went through the back door and onto the porch.

"Grandpa, dinner's ready."

Grandpa put his axe down, wiped the sweat from his brow with his hat and said to William, "Come along now. You did a good job of piling that firewood. Let's go and see what your mom has cooking for us."

Mom brushed aside some dark damp tendrils of hair from her forehead, then picked up the grumbling little bundle from her cradle and disappeared into the room adjoining the kitchen. Ellen looked after them and thought about the times her mom had spent with her, reading and talking, telling her stories about when she came to Canada from England. But there was no time for that now. It seemed that she was always busy now that her little sister, Daisy, had come along. Ellen peeked into the bedroom. Her mom had unbuttoned the front of her printed cotton dress and was contentedly gazing at the chubby little baby, who had one little fist clenched and the other openhanded on her breast. She was a little Daisy alright, with delicate pink lips that pressed against her mom's bosom.

She never talks to me like that. She likes that baby better than me, she thought.

"Ellen, come on now. Your dad's hungry, so is Grandpa. You need to get dinner on the table for them. Everything is cooked and ready. Just put it on the table, and make sure nothing is missing from the setting."

Mom went back to her restful job of feeding Daisy.

"Hey, my little jelly belly Ellie. Are you Mom's helper today?"

Ellen looked up at her dad and nodded, joyful at his approval. Her dad winked at her, and smiled.

Like a brilliant sunbeam, his blue eyes sparkled, lighting up a grin that was large and relaxed. He was always smiling, spreading warmth to those he greeted. Dark hair framed his fair skin that was turning golden from many hours working outdoors in the fields. His sweat-soaked cotton shirt was rolled up above the elbows and his trousers were held up with suspenders crossed over his lean muscular body. Dad went to the stand in the corner that held the blue metal water bucket and scooped out some cool water with a dipper into a cup. Hungrily, he quenched his hot morning's work.

Everyone washed up, and took their places at the large wooden table in the kitchen. Mom took a loaf of warm bread out of the warming oven and cut several soft thick slices off of it. On the table was a saucer with thick creamy yellow butter, inviting them to layer it on the delicate bread. As they ate, the musical sounds of contented chatter and clattering dishes filled the warm kitchen air.

William sighed and looked down at the cob of corn on his plate. Except for a few empty pockets that had been chewed, the rows of yellow kernels still marched down the hot slippery buttered cob.

He moaned, half to himself, as he said,

"I don't want corn. I don't like it."

"You've been filling up with bread and butter. You need to get started on that corn," said Mom.

"You're awfully quiet, Ellen," said Grandpa.

Ellen just looked at her plate. She ate half of her corn and fiddled with her lump of potatoes. Grandpa watched her, and smiled to himself. He wiped his white beard, being careful to keep it clean. He only shaved once a year, in the spring time, then let it grow through to the winter. When Christmas came he loved to play his annual joke on the children. He hoped that it would be a while yet before he was found out.

"You know, the saskatoons are ripe. I found some bushes down by the river. They're plumb full of juicy ripe berries," said Grandpa.

He looked right at Ellen and continued,

"I sure could use some help picking some to make jam, and maybe a pie if there's enough."

Ellen smiled and agreed with a nod. She loved going with Grandpa. He might have time to tell her some stories. Sometimes they would just lay in the grass, look at the clouds in the sky, and talk about just about everything. He was never in a hurry. She loved to hear about his adventures in Ontario before he came to Manitoba to live. He was a tall quiet man with a smile and a presence that was warm and congenial.

"After you help clean up, Ellen, you can go," said Mom.

Ellen excused herself from the table and ran out to the back porch to find two small metal buckets to pick the berries in.

"I'm a little concerned," said Dad. "She's awfully quiet."

"She'll be fine once she gets used to the idea that the world doesn't always revolve around her," said Mom.

When Ellen returned with the buckets she helped her mom clean off the table and when the large reservoir of steaming hot water in the stove was ready, the basin was filled and the dishes were washed and dried. The kitchen had a satisfying and fragrant feeling. Its walls were painted halfway up, trimmed with a railing and white-washed with calcimine. It sighed with contentment in the afternoon heat. The golden sideboard was polished and glossy, full of Mom's blue willow dishes and cutlery. By the wood-burning stove was a half-barrel on iron feet that held wood for the stove. The cooking stove was the heart of the kitchen, keeping them warm in winter as well as cooking their food and heating their water.

"Come on, Ellen. Let's go find them berries." said Grandpa.

Ellen skipped to keep up to her grandpa's long strides. Her silver bucket bobbed up and down as they walked through the wavy grass, past the lazy velvet-brown cows (their tails slowly swishing back and forth shooing away the flies on their flanks), and down the path towards the river.

The bushes they found were dripping with red-blue saskatoons, juicy and warmed by the sun. Ellen and Grandpa picked quickly, filling both their pails and their mouths. Somehow, picking berries was a pleasure when you had someone to talk to while you worked. And talk they did.

"Grandpa, were there Indians in Ontario?"

"Oh, yes, they lived there long before I did."

"Did you know any Indians?"

"Not too many, but there was one fellow, name was Alfred Longbow. Great hunter he was. He used to bring me rabbits. The Indians were quiet you know. You would never hear them coming up. You would just look up and there they were. Made you jump sometimes."

"Mom worries about them. I guess she's not used to them like dad is."

"Yup, your dad likes to trade with them. They like your dad too. He's good friends with them."

"One time an Indian was at the front door. He looked scary. His hair was long and he just stared at me. He had some long beads around his neck and a funny coat. My dad says he's a chief. What's a chief?"

"He's kinda the boss, the one everyone listens to when they need to know something."

"I was scared so I ran upstairs and shut my door."

"Well, we should head back now. Our buckets are pretty full, and so are we. Your mouth is purple, Ellie! I think you ate more than you put in your bucket."

They walked back a little slower, their pails weighed down with the succulent sweet fruit. They were happy with their afternoon outing.

"Look, Grandpa!"

"Now what in tarnation is that?"

"It's a wagon, Grandpa."

They started to walk a little faster. Curiosity was growing as they approached the road in front of their house where the wagon was stopped.

The wagon was covered with a wood structure and was carrying a variety of utensils, from pots and pans to rakes and shovels hanging from its outside. It was painted red. Tied to the back of the wagon was the most beautiful horse Ellen had ever seen. It was a rich golden colour, and its coat glowed in the sunshine. It had what looked like a white diamond on its face and two white socks on its back feet. It was pulling on the lead halter, restless to resume moving.

Ellen watched her dad talk to the peddler. Although she couldn't hear what they were saying, she saw her dad walk around to the back of the wagon. He ran his hands down the horse's back, brought its legs up and looked at its foot, then in its mouth. He seemed to be smiling as he continued his examination. Ellen could hear a muffled conversation then saw them shake hands. Her dad untied the horse and led it into the barn.

Ellen and Grandpa went into the house with their buckets of saskatoons and put them on the table for Mom to cook later. Mom was busy with Daisy again, so Ellen ran back outside. Grandpa was tired, so he decided to have a nap in his room, adjacent to the kitchen.

Once outside, Ellen was startled to hear loud squealing, a whip cracking, donkeys braying, and the peddler shouting.

"Giddap now you two, giddap! Come on now, get going, giddap!"

Then off went the wagon with one of their big sows tied to where the horse had been led, behind the wagon. Its feet were stubbornly digging into the ground, and its neck twisting to rid itself of the rope that was pulling it. The pig squealed all the way down the road as it was being led away, shattering the summer quiet with snorts and screeches. The two donkeys loped along in unison, their heads nodding in obedience to the peddler's commands.

Curious, Ellen followed her dad into the barn. She found him with the horse in a stall.

"Nice looking horse, eh, Ellen?"

"Is it ours, Dad?"

"Not ours," he said. "Yours."

"Mine!" she gasped. "But I don't know how to look after it."

"It's a she," he said. "She's a Morgan mare, a young one, like you. Don't worry, you'll learn how to take care of her."

"Here," said Dad. "Give her this. See if she likes it. Keep your hand flat."

He handed her a cob of corn with the husk off. Ellen took it and carefully offered it to the horse. The horse shook her head, her calm brown eyes were fixed on Ellen, watching, reaching down into her soul. The mare made a quiet little warble deep inside her throat. Her eyes held a soft expression in a well-proportioned head, and between her sensitive ears she was wide with intelligence. Her large nostrils promised good energy and wind.

"Come on, it's okay," Ellen whispered.

The horse leaned down, wrapped her lips around the cob, exposing her large teeth, and took it from her. She chewed largely, contently, and lazily on the corn. The cob of corn crunched as it moved from side to side in her mouth, and when it was finished she spit out the stripped cob. Then she looked Ellen over, searching with her muzzle for more treats, and softly snorting her approval.

"I think she likes me, Dad."

Ellen stretched up and stroked her smooth silky coat.

"Do you think she's thirsty?" said Ellen.

"I wouldn't be surprised," said Dad.

Ellen quickly ran and filled a bucket with fresh water from the well, brought it back and offered it to the horse. She drank noisily from the bucket.

Her dad led the mare out of her stall and out the barn door with Ellen following. The young horse was magnificently beautiful. Its silhouette outlined by the radiant sunshine was glowing against the darkness of the barn interior. Her tail was proudly held high, expressing her youthful spirit. They stopped at a railing and tied the horse. Her dad lifted Ellen up onto the horse's bare back, took the rope, and led them around in a circle.

"Now, hang on Ellie, grab her mane. There, that's right."

Then he untied the lead rope, stepped to the back and clucking a giddap, he gave her a light push forward.

The horse started off at a trot then sped up. At first Ellen was rigid with fear as the horse began to move. She laid down on the horse's back, gripping her mane and hardly daring to look around. The thundering muscular movement pulsed through her small body as the horse's hooves dug into the earth, scattering dirt and grass behind them. Fear dissolved into excitement as their bodies began to move as one. Her grasp on the mane tightened, determination settling into her. She felt as though she was flying on an angel's wings. The horse circled around through the field of tall grass, corralled by the wooden fence surrounding it. She was on her way back when she started to trot again. Ellen's joyful heart raced. She was light headed and giddy when they returned to her dad.

Ellen leaned into the horse, her mouth close to her ear, and she whispered,

"Nell. I'm going to call you Nell. I love you, Nell."

Chapter 2
A Prairie Fire

Ellen lifted her head up from the garden she was weeding. She moaned as her back straightened out, and she stretched. She was sick of pulling weeds from around the blue-green Brussels sprouts and the long row of carrots.

I hate this job! I'd much rather be helping Dad and William with the animals, or riding Nell. I don't think I'll ever get this done, and it'll be full of weeds again next week. Why do girls have to do girl stuff anyways?" she thought. Boys' stuff is so much more fun. Mom keeps telling me that I need to act like a lady. She wants me to learn how to cook and clean the house but that's no fun. I can handle my horse as well as any boy can.

She sniffed the air, then saw the glow in the distance. At the same time she noticed a group of green grasshoppers, previously hidden, scurrying out from underneath the cabbage leaves where she had been working. They were clicking and jumping erratically about her feet.

She looked at her hands now grimy from working in the rich earth, then carefully reached up and removed her damp straw hat. Wiping her sweaty face with the back of her hand, she stood up and squinted into the sunshine to get a better look at what was in the distance. As if a warning bell was ringing, a flock of sparrows, chattering excitedly, rose up in unison into the air. Released from the bushes they were living in, they scattered and flew east. Two fluffy fat grey rabbits were hopping as fast as their little legs could carry them, out of the grasses and down the pathway away from the rosy glow in the sky, close to the horizon, and west of the farm. In the next field two white tailed deer appeared, stopped, looked around, then bounded full speed towards the road going east. Following them was a young fawn struggling to keep up to the older deer. Tell-tale grey smoke curled up into the sky.

Daisy was inside the farmhouse with Mom. She was now six years old and mature enough to help, first picking beans and washing them, and then taking out the compost when Mom had finished cutting them up. She wasn't a strong child, much thinner and smaller than Ellen. Her complexion was fair with soft pale cheeks, accentuated by the contrast of dark curly hair. Her mom loved to comb her thick curly hair and on this day it was done up in two ponytails with pink ribbons to match her cotton dress. Daisy was content to play indoors with her hand made doll, Molly, changing the clothes that she and Mom had made for her, and rocking her in the little cradle Grandpa made. Mom was bustling around her kitchen with glass jars and their lids bubbling on the wood stove in preparation for canning freshly picked green beans. The day was hotter than usual, and she wondered about the wisdom of tackling the job of preserving beans when it was warm, but she felt they couldn't wait another day. They were already starting to over-ripen on the plants. She was working diligently, with sweat dripping down her brow and into her deep blue eyes. Her loose yellow cotton dress stuck in places to her damp body, but absorbed her body heat as she worked.

Dad and Grandpa were out checking the fields of corn and potatoes when they noticed the glow, and then the smoke in the late August sky.

"I don't like the look of that," said Dad.

The scent of new growth in full bloom was polluted with the of a dirty cloud of smutty smoke that smeared and tarnished the wide sky above them.

"You'd better head home and get help. I'm going to see where the fire is and what can be done."

The worry on Dad's face deepened as he thought about his family at the farmhouse only a short distance away.

While Grandpa hurried back, Dad started to walk along the fence line over a hill, then broke into a jog as he raced to find the source of the fire. His heart was pounding and his thoughts were jumbled as he hardly dared to grasp what possibly lay ahead. His every sense told him what he would find, what every prairie farmer dreads. Fire! It was already burning the dry grasses and spitting out flames in its path. In his neighbour's pasture over the rise of the hill he could hear, then see, the Jones family beating at the flames and barking out orders for more water.

Dad saw that they were working hard to put the fire out in their fields. But he also saw that the wind was changing and blowing the flames towards him. As the fire grew, it burned passionately, torturing the fields, and moving snakelike across the ground. The dry grasses sparked and cracked in the heat while the hungry red flames devoured and cleansed the crops in the fields. As the fiery wall grew larger, the smoke filled the air with black and sparkling red ashes. There was a resounding roar that seemed to be impossible to contain. His ears ached in response to the noise. His face was already red and sweating in the wicked heat.

With a burst, the kitchen door flew open and Grandpa rushed in. His eyes were wide with excitement and worry.

"Hurry, Kate. There's a fire in the west section. It's coming from the Jones' farm next to us along the railroad track. We need Ellen to take Daisy to the Stuart farm and get help to put the fire out."

"Oh my god! How bad is it?"

"Bad! The wind is up and it's blowing this way. Hurry, there's no time to talk. Where are Ellen and William? Billy's already out there but he needs help fast."

"Ellen's in the garden. Last I saw him, William went to feed the chickens."

"Go and find William and Ellen. I'm going to hitch up the wagon."

After turning the damper on the stove down, Mom ran out the front door and yelled:

"Ellen, come quickly. Your dad needs help. There's a fire!"

Ellen followed her mom out to the chicken coop to find William. His chickens were beautiful fluffy Rhode Island Reds, their burnt red and burgundy velvet feathers flamed in the sunlight.

"William, William, where are you? Come quickly!"

William appeared from out of the door of the coup with a chicken perched high on his shoulder.

He was carrying a basketful of brown eggs that he had gathered for Mom.

"Where's the smoke coming from? Where's Dad?"

"The west section. There's a prairie fire started. Your dad's already there. He needs help right away."

"Oh, no! Are my chickens going to burn?"

"No, of course not. But hurry. We all need to help."

In the barn, Grandpa was busy putting the harnesses on their two dark Belgian horses. They were reacting to the tension, sensing that something wasn't right, whinnying and shaking their heads, their feet restless and skittish, as Grandpa led them out and hitched them to their wooden wagon. The curled smoke was getting larger in the sky, clouding over and changing the atmosphere from a clear blue to hazy grey. The wagon would carry buckets of water to help Dad put the fire out or at least stop it from spreading. Ellen harnessed Nell up to the cart. The horse's sensitive nose was lifting in the air in response to the smoke that was advancing. Aware that there was an emergency, Nell was anxious to get moving.

"Easy girl, easy. We'll be all right. We just have to get you hitched so we can go for help."

"Ellen, take Daisy with you in the cart and head for the Stuart farm. Leave Daisy with them and tell them we need help right away," said Mom.

When Ellen got the horse and cart ready she turned to pick up Daisy to put her into the cart beside her, but she wasn't there.

"Come on, Daisy. Let's go!" she shouted, getting anxious to head down the road.

Daisy was running back into the house as Ellen was calling her. Ellen hung onto her halter reins and talked quietly in Nell's ear, trying to reassure an agitated Nell and keep her from bolting.

"Daisy, come back. We need to go!"

"Not without Molly," she replied, and through the screen door she went.

William and Mom went into the house and Mom returned with Daisy carrying her doll, Molly. She lifted her into the cart and without any more conversation, Ellen slapped the reins and urged Nell on, until she was galloping towards their neighbour's house, with Daisy, Molly and Ellen all safely inside the cart.

At the house, Mom and William gathered up burlap gunny sacks that once held flour and sugar. The sacks that were stored at the back of the cow barn were piled in layers in the wagon, with barrels filled with water from the well and some shovels, picks and the plough. Then the three of them drove the wagon downhill a mile across the quarter section of fields to help Dad.

Mom, William and Grandpa arrived in the wagon a few minutes later. They left the wagon a safe distance away, then dunked the sacks in the water and started beating the fields to put out the fire. While they were doing this, Dad was busy digging a trench to make a backfire, a strip of burned ground, so the fire wouldn't jump to the next field. He hitched the horses to the plough and dug furiously with super human energy, praying that he would be able to stop the advance of the demonic monster. Mom and William furiously pounded the sparking grasses with wet sacks, dunking and wringing them with water every so often when they were dry again. They both had shoes on their feet but the merciless fire simmering under the grass blackened the soles of them. Their faces were red and burning, and sweat dripped down as they worked with frenzied energy. The swirling smoke invaded their stinging eyes, while the taste of it hung in their parched throats.

At the farmhouse, wagons quickly came bumping in. The Saunders and the McDonalds, along with the Reids, arrived ready to assist, with shovels and sacks to help put the fire out. Some wagons were full of precious water-filled barrels. They drove past the farmhouse, down the pathway, and out into the burning fields.

Nell came behind them, with Ellen driving the cart. She'd left Daisy at the Stuarts, but decided that she was perfectly capable of helping too. After all, she was older than William, and he was out there helping Mom and Dad.

I'm going to help put the fire out, she thought, and followed the parade of neighbours armed with whatever they could find to fight the prairie fire.

When Ellen and Nell arrived at the burning fields, she checked the disappearing water in the barrels that were in their wagon and decided to fill them again at the edge of the river half of a mile north of the raging stretch of land. She dragged the smaller barrels and a bucket and put them in the cart that Nell was pulling, flicked the reins and off she went in that direction. She pulled in close to the riverbank, and while Nell waited, she grabbed her bucket and made her way through the path dividing the bushes to the river. The water was gurgling and rushing past her but she managed to kneel and fill her bucket up with water, then headed back with it to the cart and poured it in the barrel. Back she went for another bucket full. She was so intent on her job that she didn't notice that the wind had changed. The fire had spread its arms out and was following behind her like a tidal wave, rapidly advancing towards the river.

When she returned to Nell and the cart, she was terrified to see the fire running towards her, its fiery breath panting and hot. She realized that she was cut off from returning the way she came, so she climbed into the cart and shook the reins and they made their way down the path of the river. It was no use. There was fire everywhere. Pockets of fire exploded in every direction she tried. When she found an opening to the river, she drove Nell and the cart right into a shallow part. She couldn't wade into the water because of the large rocks and swirling deep currents, so she started to look for another way to get out. As she looked back, she saw the flames climb the trees, and with a searing shriek incinerate them almost instantly. The heat was as intense as her terrible fear. She started to move forward at the edge of the water but was startled at first by a loud crack, then a burning tree trunk fell in front of her blocking her way forward. With her heart racing, she backed up and gingerly found her way around it.

How will I get out, she thought desperately.

Nell, oh Nell, what did I do?

Talking to herself, she said, "There's got to be a way. Don't panic. Keep looking."

She tried several times to find a way past the flames, fear gripping her young heart. Nell started to whinny and shake her head. Her eyes were wild with worry, and her nostrils flared as the smoke assaulted her nose and eyes. Her ears twitched at the roar of the fire. The water in the river had felt cool next to Ellen's baking skin, and she finally realized what she needed to do, what Nell wanted her to do. She quickly unhitched Nell from the cart and climbed on her back, and the horse found her way into the cold water. With Ellen on her bare back, Nell swam to the middle of the river. The inferno-like fire was blazing on the shore around them. Ellen dunked her head under the water and hung on to Nell's mane for dear life. The water rushed past her and through her. Her exhaled bubbles mixed with the frothy white water, soaking her pores and playing with her swirling hair. She came up gasping for air to a pink and black world, her eyes bleary. She sucked some air into her aching lungs then went under again. She didn't know how long she and Nell had stayed there or how many times she had dunked her head but gradually she became aware that Nell was standing on stable ground on the river bottom and solidly planted there, up to her neck in water. The cold water rushed past Nell's neck, flicking her wet mane and both girl and horse escaped the flames. Nell held firm and brave while Ellen, who was tired and frightened, clung to her muscular body. She prayed that she and Nell would get out of there alive and that her family was all right.

Exhaustion set in to the group of prairie people pounding the fire out. They continued on until the last spark was out and only a stale smoky fog hung like a drape over the charcoal desert that was once green and gold fields. Silently their friends and neighbours made their way back to the road that led them to their homes, their clothes in tatters and their faces and hands blackened and made sweaty by the dirty smoke. Many stopped to offer a comforting touch on Mom's shoulder. Mom, Grandpa, and William climbed into the wagon and started home. Thoughts of home and whether it was still there, kept them silent on the ride towards their farmhouse. Fear turned to relief when they came over the hill and their red brick house and the barns, fields and gardens were still there untouched by the flames.

Dad's feet crunched the brittle stalks of wheat and they disintegrated and snapped into ashes as he walked the length of the fields, inspecting the extent of the damage. The fire was extinguished but the heavy silence was eerie after the deafening roar of the wildfire was exhausted.

He leaned down to look at the crisp burnt and twisted piece of inky charcoal that was once green and nourishing. There was a frown on his face as weariness gave way to despair but there was always hope that over the hill it wouldn't be so badly devastated, and so he kept walking. The fire had devoured his most western fields of wheat, oats and corn. The dead grey stalks stared back at him in shock at the brutal slayings. He kept walking the half mile towards the river where the corpses of burnt bushes and trees lined the shores of the water. He barely noticed his own thirst and fatigue, his face and arms black with soot and sweat. As he slowly made his way down the side of the river his attention was drawn to something in the water close to the shore. It was an object the size of a cart. He started to run and trembling couldn't believe his eyes when he got close. It was a cart. His cart.

How'd this get here? he thought. A slow realization crept into his tired body. Ellen! Where is she? She can't be here.

He broke into an adrenal run and hoarsely called her name, all the while praying that he was wrong. She had to be back at the farmhouse.

Then he heard it. Nell. Nell was whinnying. It was Nell.

"Ellen! Where are you?"

He stopped and heard her answer in a weakened small voice.

"Daddy, Daddy. Please help me!"

He looked up and saw them, still in the water, with Ellen laying on Nell's back and clinging to her mane. Dad whistled and Nell answered. She turned with a jerk and started to walk, then swim to the charred shore where Dad was. Dad waded out as far as he could go and when he could reach Nell's reins he grabbed hold and led the horse and girl back to the shore. Ellen's blue hands were frozen in their grip on Nell's mane and Dad had to rub them and coax her to let go. She fell into his arms and her dad held her tightly in a huge emotional embrace.

"Dad, I'm so sorry."

"It's okay, girl. You're okay, we're all okay." His voice broke and he let out a tired sigh and his dry burning eyes filled up with tears of relief.

Back at home, Grandpa unhitched the Belgian horses from the wagon and led them into the barn.

"William, get me some water for these horses."

William did as he was asked, even though he was tired enough to go right to sleep without even eating.

Mom looked at the gunny sacks that were burnt and in tatters.

Oh well, she thought as she examined some of them. The burnt charcoal smell was too much for her to bear so she threw the rags just inside the barn to be dealt with later. Mom wearily dragged herself into the house.

Jenny Stuart drove up with Daisy in her buggy.

When Jenny saw Grandpa walking towards her she stopped to ask if they were able to get the fire out.

"I believe so," he replied.

"Thank you for looking after Daisy. Isn't Ellen with you, too?"

"No, she left right away. She said that she was going to help put the fire out."

"I didn't see her there."

He turned and walked back into the barn to see if she or Nell were there. His steps quickened as possibilities began to enter his mind. Nell's stall was empty and Ellen was nowhere to be found. He ran as quickly as his tired old bones would let him to the farmhouse and rushed through the door.

"Kate, Kate! Is Ellen in the house?"

"No, I thought she was with Daisy at the Stuart farm."

Jenny followed him in with Daisy and told Mom that Ellen wasn't with her and that she had left right away to help put the fire out. Confusion settled in. William looked upstairs and everyone was calling Ellen hoping for an answer to their pleas. A sick feeling settled into Mom and rose up into her throat as the panic started to rise. Grandpa's shoulders drooped lower each time Ellen didn't answer and the lines in his face deepened.

They went outside to check around the garden and the chicken coop with fear rising like the evening tide, while minutes felt like hours in their search. William's call broke the tension in the air.

"Mom, Grandpa. Look! I think it's them coming."

Over the hill slowly walking towards them was a dark silhouette of a man leading a horse, and yes, there was a rider on the horse. They walked, then ran ahead to meet them. Ellen looked like a wet rag shivering, her hair wet and plastered to her head and still cold from the water in the river.

"Is she okay, Billy?" said Mom.

"Yes, she's okay. Cold, but okay."

Grandpa let out a sigh of relief allowing the anxiety to escape while Mom gave Ellen a hug. Even though Dad was bone tired he led Nell into her stall, gave her some fresh hay to sleep on and food and water. He stroked her neck and whispered, "Thanks, Nell. You did a good job."

Once inside the farmhouse, Ellen was wrapped in warm blankets and Mom put vaseline on all of their burning faces. She made hot broth and they all gathered around for some nourishment, glad that at least their family was all together in spite of the terrible fire.

Chapter 3
School Days

The cool morning air was bright through her small window. The baby blue and yellow dawn tickled the pink and blue patchwork quilt her mom had made. Her quilt and the flannelette sheets were snugly wrapped around her and her sister, Daisy. Sunlight speckled the pink rosebud and green leaf pattern on the wallboard that decorated their bedroom. Outside a white leghorn rooster was calling the farm's occupants to rise, and in the distance she could hear her dad talking to the barn animals as he fed and watered them. She heard the door open and close in the kitchen and knew that her dad had returned from doing barn chores. Ellen wasn't ready to leave the comfort of her sister's warmth and the wooden bed that Grandpa had made, so she snuggled down underneath pretending that it was still night time. But the smell of porridge, fresh bread and homemade vegetable soup cooking, and her mom calling her, finally drew her to her feet on the homemade oval braided rug covering the cool wooden floor. Outside, the farm was clothed in a coverlet of frost sparkling like diamonds. It announced an end to the ripe activity of summer. She shivered into her scratchy wool leggings and socks, and pulled her dress over her head wondering if she should also wear her long underwear, finally deciding that she wouldn't need to today.

"Come on, Daisy. It's time to get up. Dad says we can take Nell to school today. We'll have fun riding in our cart."

She looked forward to Nell pulling them in the wooden cart and being in charge of the reins. It was more fun than walking the four miles to their one room schoolhouse, and at the end of the day walking home again, their lunch kits swinging back and forth in one hand and their bundles of books under the other arm. The children didn't mind the walk. They had time to skip stones, tease each other and watch for frogs and gophers along the way to school and back. Jackets were discarded and carried as they meandered their way home. It became colder, however, so Dad decided that Nell would take the three children to school because the weather was becoming more unpredictable.

Daisy pulled the covers over her head, pretending not to hear her while Ellen finished dressing.

When Daisy started to stir, Ellen bounded down the narrow stairs, and turned the corner towards the kitchen. She stopped and listened when she heard her parents speaking to each other. As they talked in the kitchen the concern in their voices was evident.

"That government agent was here again yesterday, Kate."

"Why does he keep bothering us? He knows we don't have the money."

"Oh, I know. But there's no use in fretting too much."

"Can we come up with the money?"

"Well, there is some grain saved from the fire and there's always the cream we send to Winnipeg. Trouble is, we'll have to settle it by next summer. We're already late with our payment."

"Do you think we could sell something?"

He paused and thought for a moment.

"Let's not worry about that yet. Don't worry, Kate, we'll figure it all out. We'll get things settled before the new baby arrives."

"By the way, William wants to go with Grandpa today."

"And miss school, I suppose. He needs to go to school."

"Ah, Kate, the boy is learning all he needs to know, about farming that is. He's good with the cattle and already is working hard, helping with the harvesting. He can read and write real well. As far as Grandpa is concerned, I don't know what those two have got planned."

"Fishing, probably. Billy, I know he's a big help on the farm but he can go with Grandpa later. He'd better get ready and go with the girls. School is more important right now."

With that, Mom went to the bottom of the stairs and called, "William, hurry up. Your breakfast is ready. School starts soon."

The children finished their breakfast of crushed wheat drowned in thick yellow cream and brown sugar, bundled up in their warm coats, toques and mittens, picked up their lunches of hot soup and sandwiches, and headed out the door towards the barn. Dad was there hitching up Nell to the little cart that they rode to school in. It had one seat in the middle and two large wheels, one on either side. The three of them crowded in together on the seat, Daisy in between William and Ellen. Her dad said to her,

"Now, Ellie, she's your pony so you take good care of her. She needs to be watered and have a bit of a walk at lunch time. Don't forget, and be careful on the road to school. Those gophers have made messes everywhere."

Ellen took the reins, and with a wave goodbye, off they went bumping down the grass and pebble pathway towards Rae school, the wheels of the cart crunching the frost and scratching the ground. The cool air was shocking to the exposed skin on their faces. The bracing ride was everything it promised to be, past some of the harvested ochre and green fields, the ones that escaped the prairie fire last summer and other fields that were charred and crisp, deadened by the leaping flames. They went past shrubs and trees turned golden with the approaching winter, while others were stripped black skeletons reaching in agony up to the sky. Oblivious to the ruin around them, the children joked and talked to Nell as she trotted along, her harness jingling in time with her steps.

"Got a crush on George, don't you, Ellie?"

"Do not! He's a creep. Anyways, I hate boys."

"Even me?"

"Only when you talk me into doing your chores so you can go fishing."

"Oh my gosh, Ellie. There's a spider on your shoulder!"

"EEEK! Get it off! William, don't do that when I'm driving! It's dangerous."

William laughed with satisfaction while his sister regained her focus.

"Ah, Nell knows where she's going. Don't you, Nell?"

Nell shook her head and softly whinnied in agreement.

"Wish I could have gone fishing today instead of going to school."

"Never mind, William. You'd better do what Mom says."

Nell pulled the cart with her charges in it all the way to school, and when they arrived, Miss Larson, fresh-faced and pretty in her royal blue dress, was on the front steps of the school ringing the hand held school bell. Their little school had been built on donated land five years ago by volunteers in the community. Standing proudly beside the schoolhouse was the community hall, a home for local dances and social gatherings. The warm-hearted two-story school stood proudly waiting to welcome its dozen students. Their mom was on the school board the previous year, and they had hired Miss Larson for her first term after normal school. William thought that she was the prettiest young lady he'd ever seen, and found himself tongue-tied when she questioned him about his school work.

"Hurry up, children. School is starting."

Ellen, William, and Daisy got out of the cart. William and Daisy ran inside with their lunches in their hands while Ellen unhitched Nell and led her into the barn behind the school. She put her into her stall and gave her some water, stroked her neck and gave her a carrot she kept in her pocket.

"There's a girl, Nell. You gave us a good ride. You wait here and be patient. I'll be back before you know it at lunchtime."

Ellen patted her while Nell nuzzled her and nodded her head, her large dark eyes reflecting hers as if to say, don't worry. I'll be right here till you get back.

Ellen found her desk in the little classroom. There were barely a dozen students there from Grade 1 to Grade 8. Her only companion in Grade 8 was a boy named George who was from the farm 15 miles south of hers. George was a freckle-faced boy with dirty blonde hair and green eyes. Ellen considered him a pest. He was continually pulling at her softly curled ponytail and poking her with his ruler.

Glowing at the back of the classroom stood the warm wood stove that kept the students comfortable and cozy during the day, and heated their homemade soup at lunch time. Pinned to the side wall, underneath the colourful caricatures of the alphabet, were illustrated stories written about their families. On the other side was a large map of the world.

In the morning, math questions written on their large black chalkboard were worked out on black slates. With perfect penmanship, Ellen wrote her Social Studies notes in her book. She loved school.

It was a chance to learn about the rest of the world, and at night she did her homework and got lost in stories and adventures that she read by the light of a coal oil lamp.

At the end of the school day, Ellen went to hitch Nell up to their cart again. Even though she had walked Nell at lunch time, Nell was quivering with anticipation, eager to be heading home to her dinner and bed of warm hay. The three of them climbed in and off they went home on the same path that they had come on. Ellen soon started to lose control as Nell knew she was heading home to her stall. Her ears pricked up and she sniffed the air in the graying late afternoon.

"Hang on, Daisy," said Ellen. "Nell knows where she's going."

"Yippee!" cried William. "Go, Nell. Go!"

The cart hit a bump when its wheel struck a large rock on the path. Ellen looked down and saw to her horror that the wheel on her side was wobbling badly. It was just barely hinged to the cart and the wobbles were getting bigger and bigger. The four miles was covered quickly as Nell, now in charge, raced home to her barn. The children hung on to the sides of the cart as they sped down the pathway towards the now twinkling light in their farmhouse.

Everyone was quiet, trusting Nell to carry them home before the wheel came right off. Nell pulled them up to the barn door and stopped and snorted, shaking her head for someone to come and unhitch her. She was hungry and ready to bed down for the night.

"It's a good thing this didn't come off. I'll fix this tonight, before you go to school tomorrow morning." Dad looked at it a little closer, then commented, "It needs a nut and a washer. I guess it was lost on the trip home. That's dangerous riding in it like that. Why didn't you stop and look at it, William?"

William's smile faded.

"She wouldn't stop, Dad! Nell just wanted to get home."

"Well, I want you to help me fix it tonight so you understand how the wheel works."

William had been so carried away and excited about the wild ride home it really hadn't occurred to him that he should stop.

"Better go see if Mom needs some help with dinner, Ellen."

Once inside the house, Ellen was surprised to see, from the kitchen window, Mr. Beettle talking to her dad at the barn door. A heavy lump formed in her chest when she saw Nell being led out of the barn and Mr. Beetle looking her over, checking her feet and mouth. He was talking to her dad while he was looking at Nell. He was shorter than her dad with a waistline that ballooned beneath his red wool jacket, stretching the bottom buttons undone. His three day old beard framed a Cheshire cat grin that was pasted on his round fleshy face. There were dark holes in his mouth where teeth once were. She could see him scratching his face as he responded to her dad. Ellen didn't like him, and certainly didn't want him around her Nell.

William came up behind her, and seeing Mr. Beetle through the window, teased,

"Oh, there's that Mr. Blubberbutt. Hope he goes away. Grandpa says he's a cheat."

Ellen didn't answer. She was too worried about what the man wanted. The morning conversation between her parents kept coming back to her. He'd better not want Nell. She let out her breath when she saw him walk to his wagon, climb in, and drive down the road. She tried not to think about it through dinner, and had difficulty going to sleep that night.

In the weeks that followed, the snow began to fall, sometimes lightly, then heavier, building snow drifts along the road to school. The sky turned to gray and the large flakes that covered the sky were blinding so that Ellen was unable to see further than Nell up ahead. Nell continued to take them to school, but not in a cart. In the snow, she pulled them in a sleigh, forging a path and tunneling through the heavy snow only to have to forge it again on the way home. The sleigh had jingle bells on it, and they could be heard in the winter air as Nell trotted along through the drifts. She always knew where she was and where she was going, bringing the children safely home from school. Sometimes a horse's eyelashes would freeze on them, so Ellen had to be careful with her best friend, Nell, and make sure that in severe cold weather Nell wore protectors for her eyes.

Saturday morning came, the sky was clear and no snow had fallen for a week. Ellen got ready and helped her dad put the saddle on Nell. She looked forward to her seven mile ride to Pratt to get the mail. The leather carrying pouch was attached to the saddle. Ellen mounted and, after saying goodbye to her dad, started off down the road south to the little town where the train station and the general store with the post office were located. The air was crisp against her face, her lungs aching, as she and Nell at first trotted, then galloped down the road. Ellen felt the freedom of an unrestrained burst of energy that only a girl, a horse, an open road and a young spirit could arouse.

"Whoa," she said to Nell and pulled on the reins as they approached the station. The train station was a wooden framed structure, painted a smart brick red and trimmed with a soft yellow. It had three gables and the upstairs housed the Station Master and his family. Outside, the roof extensions reached over the wooden platform that offered patrons some protection from the weather. The train was an important connector for far-reaching farms in the area. Shipments of grain, dairy products and general goods arrived and left by the train that followed the cold metal tracks that stretched across the prairies as far as the eye could see.

Someday I'm going to travel on this. I'd really like to see what the rest of the country looks like, especially cities like Winnipeg and maybe even Toronto she thought.

Beside the train station sat the grain elevator. This prairie princess, dressed in CPR red was a giant reaching up to the sky. Its purpose was to feed the steaming trains with the farmers' wheat and transport it to the flour mills where it would be processed. The flour would then be shipped to other parts of the world.

Nell trotted past the large gasping steel train to the general store behind the station, knowing very well where to stop: right in front of the general store. The store was also a wooden building with two large windows in the front, a wide front porch with a sign hung at the front of it saying: PRATT GENERAL STORE.

Ellen tied Nell to the post and bounded up the wooden stairs. Ellen was confident and sure-footed, even though the stairs were still a bit icy after being swept clean of the snow. Inside the store was a kaleidoscope of shapes and colors. There were shelves full of canned goods, bolts of material, tins of coffee and tea, sacks of sugar, and candy in jars that lined the counter.

"Hello there, Ellen," said Mr. Peterson. "Come for your mail?"

"Yup," said Ellen. "Are there any letters or parcels?"

"There sure are. A letter came just this morning on the train. Letter's all the way from England. I think it's for your mother."

"Is there any more?"

"Ah, yeah, there's a letter here from Winnipeg for your father. That's about it this week."

"Thanks," said Ellen, and she turned to leave with the letters.

Mr. Peterson called after her,

"Say, it's a long ride from home for a young girl. I have some peppermint candy that's just waiting to be eaten. How about a piece to take home with you? Take two more for your brother and sister.

And say hi to your mom and dad for me."

"Thank you," said Ellen without any hesitation.

The sky was clouding over, with gray and white snow clouds settling in as they started down the road back home. Nell was moving at a good pace through the falling snow, and Ellen was deep in thought about Christmas, which wasn't too far away. She was jerked to attention by the sudden bolt by Nell, and the unexpected action that stopped her threw Ellen over her head and right into a snow bank. She hit the icy wet wall of snow with a thud.

Nell whinnied and started to circle around Ellen. She nudged her with her muzzle and whinnied some more but there was no response from Ellen. She remained motionless while the flurries of snow started to cover her. Nell, understanding that Ellen was hurt, whinnied and prodded to try to get her up again. After what seemed like a long time, Ellen began to stir but the cold caused her to shiver uncontrollably as the ice dripped down her jacket front and her pants and into her boots.

As awareness returned, she remembered where she was, slowly got up, shook off her clothes and rubbed her hands together to try to warm them. She checked that the leather pouch was still there, then took the reins that were hanging from Nell's head close to her. Nell was still whinnying as if trying to tell her something.

"What's wrong, girl?" said Ellen.

Ellen led her a few feet and could see that Nell had a limp.

"You must have stepped into a hole," she said.

She ran her hand up and down Nell's leg but couldn't find anything wrong, so she took her reins and walked beside her, gently nudging Nell forward. Ellen's legs and hands were shaky and lacking the carefree confidence she had enjoyed earlier. Her vision was blurred by the blinding snow and the road home now concealed with snow drifts had become anonymous.

Home," she thought. We need to get home.

Suddenly, she was overcome with a longing for the warmth and safety of her family's farmhouse. There was a faint flutter in the pit of her stomach that she tried to ignore and bravely she moved ahead, one foot in front of the other.

"Where are we, Nell? I hope we're going the right way. We have to keep moving, Nell."

The large snowflakes that were drifting down from the grey blanket in the sky were blinding. Ellen kept blinking away the cold still moving wall of white and grey that surrounded her and Nell.

Anxiety rose up in her throat but was forced down again as she talked softly to both Nell and herself. Her feet and fingers, that were tight around the reins, ached with icy coldness.

"Just keep moving. There's a girl, Nell. We're going to get home all right."

Nell and Ellen kept walking, Nell leading and giving Ellen some protection from the icy wind and freezing snowfall. The two of them trudged ahead slowly but determined, mindful of Nell's injury. Their journey was long and sharp through the thick snow. They were almost home when Ellen saw someone riding towards them. The silhouette was barely visible through the hazy white cloak of the flurries.

"Dad!" she cried.

"Ellen. Thank goodness. We were worried when you didn't come back right away."

"I think Nell is hurt, Dad."

"All right, let's get you both home."

After checking Nell's leg, he lifted Ellen onto the back of his horse, Sal, took Nell's reins, and walking, led Nell and Ellen home.

Chapter 4
Christmas Magic

"Ouch! Stop that!"

Ellen jumped and her blue eyes squinted in response to the elastic band that nicked the back of her head. She rubbed it with her hand and turned around to see George behind her. He was wearing a silly grin and looked around in an irritatingly confident manner. Ellen pursed her lips and with her nose in the air she turned back to face the front. Miss Larson stopped conducting the music practice, looked directly at Ellen and asked, "Is there a problem, Ellen? You need to pay attention and not disrupt the class when we're rehearsing."

Ellen didn't answer. She just looked down and out of the corner of her eyes scowled back at George.

They only had a week before their school's annual Christmas concert. Both the school children and their parents looked forward to it. It was a celebration that lightened the dark days of winter and marked the beginning of school holidays for the month of January. With gusto they sang, *"The Twelve Days of Christmas."* Each student was assigned a line to sing. Together they sang,

"On the first day of Christmas my true love sent to me."

Mary sang out with a clear voice,

"a partridge in a pear tree."

"On the second day of Christmas my true love sent to me," the class joined in.

"Two turtle doves," Ellen sang.

"and a partridge in a pear tree," sang Mary.

When it was his turn, George sang,

"six geese a laying."

He sang off key and the "laying" came out in the high pitched squawk of a frustrated chicken when William elbowed him in the ribs. The boys giggled and pushed at each other in the back row. They were standing in two rows at the front of the class. Ellen was on the outside of the first row with her sister, Daisy, beside her.

Mary, with short blonde hair and green eyes was in Grade 5, and her little sister, Helen, who was the same age as Daisy and Mabel, a tall girl with dark tightly curled hair, was beside them. Joy and Sarah who were best friends, and both in Grade 6, stood beside William and George in the back row. James, a small quiet boy in Grade 4, and the red headed twins, Joseph and Raymond from Grade 3, fidgeted behind at the far side of the group.

Little Daisy sang the high notes of *"five golden rings"* so sweetly that it was like angel's breath twirling in a breeze. They finished the song with the whole class singing a long, drawn-out *"and a partridge in a pear tree."*

Miss Larson dropped her arms, looked around, and said,

"That sounded good. But remember to sing out nice and full so everyone can hear you in the hall. Mrs. Saunders will accompany you on the piano, so you need to sing out. Now, the last song that we need to practice is *"Silent Night,"* but it's getting late and you need to start home, so we'll practice it on Monday. Class, I want you to be sure to memorize your lines in the pageant. Daisy, don't forget: We'll need Molly to be the baby Jesus. William, make sure you practice your recital. Okay, that's all. Class dismissed."

The chairs and desks scratched the floor as they were pushed back into place, and some scattered notebooks were piled inside their desks while others were gathered up to be brought home. The noises of the children putting on their overcoats and boots and talking to each other quickly died down. The daytime glow of the fire in the stove at the back of the classroom died away to crimson hot embers.

The little schoolhouse quietly settled in for a winter's night sleep. Ellen deliberately ignored George and hurried out to the barn to hitch Nell up to their sleigh. She was almost done when a smiling George appeared around the corner.

"You sound just like six geese singing," Ellen taunted.

"What do you mean?" said George, his smile turning to a frown.

"I mean a frog could sing better than you."

"Could not! At least I'm not a freckle face!" he exploded.

"I'm not a freckle face," Ellen retorted.

"You've got freckles all over you."

"I've got freckles! You should see yourself!"

"And look at those stupid boots you're wearing. They look like work boots."

"Will you just get lost, George," Ellen screeched at him. Her cheeks turned a bright pink as the heat began to rise up from her neck to the top of her head.

"Yeah, yeah. I'm going. Soon's I get my horse hitched up."

Ellen grabbed Nell's reins and stomped out, leading Nell out of the barn door. Nell's tail was swinging high, her snorts sounding as ruffled as Ellen's wounded ego.

Outside the lonely schoolhouse and community hall beside it looked like two brightly coloured postage stamps against the ivory hills. Its breathing slowed down while it watched the children follow the roads back to their farms. They were radiant, haloed with bright golden light beaming from the evening sun. The icy snow sparkled and shimmered as daylight was about to give way to darkness.

Ellen was sulky and hardly spoke to William and Daisy on the ride home. Her ears were ringing with George's taunts.

"Come on, Ellie. Watch what you're doing!" William said, but Ellen didn't answer him. Only Nell's jingle bells were heard in the crisp cold air as they trotted towards home. The clear sky gave way to the foggy haze of snow clouds and large snowflakes that began to fall. Some stuck to her eyelashes, crusted her warm woolen toque and dripped, cold and wet from her gloved hands and leather reins.

Later that night, Ellen snuck out to the barn before anyone noticed. She managed to leave the kitchen before the hot water was ready to wash the dishes with.

William or Daisy can help Mom she thought.

Ellen picked up the curry comb that was beside the saddle and started to curry Nell. She used large vigorous circular motions that combed out any dirt on her coat, leaving it a glossy brown. She had to be careful of sensitive areas around her belly and between her back legs. The hard work started to ease some of the tension out of her. Nell was contented with the brushing, and with listening to Ellen's grumbles.

"I don't have freckles. And there's nothing wrong with my boots. Is there Nell?"

Nell looked back at her with eyes that were a liquid mirror, connecting to Ellen's. Nell softly whinnied and shook her head. Ellen found comfort brushing Nell's silky coat. Her hand was damp against the wooden handle of the curry comb while the other hand smoothed Nell's warm and silky body.

"Honestly, boys are such a pain. I'm glad that you're not a boy."

Nell nodded in agreement.

When both Ellen and Nell were soothed from the grooming, Ellen quietly went back into the house.

Grandpa was standing in the parlour with William and Daisy. His curly white beard had grown long and reached down his neck. His blue eyes twinkled and peeked out from beneath his bushy white eyebrows and gently-lined face. Keeping him warm was his worsted brown wool jacket, the front pocket beautified with the rich gold chain of his pocket watch. He would happily pull out the watch, flip open the cover and check the time when someone asked him, "What time is it?"

Animated and radiant, he recited, "*'Twas the Night Before Christmas.*" Grandpa loved to recite poetry. His voice was deep and clear, and he spoke with so much expression you could almost see Santa coming down the chimney with gifts for everyone. William was sitting erect on the large comfortable blue sofa, watching and listening very closely, with a sunny smile that spread across his young face. His gilded hair sparkled in the low illumination of the oil lamp. Even the bright flowered wallpaper, now shadowed in the evening light, seemed to nod in approval at the joyful noise circulating within its walls.

Daisy in her hand knit green wool sweater and warm pants over wool stockings, rocked her doll, Molly, in its cradle, then picked her up and held her close while she listened to Grandpa's recitation. Ellen listened for a while then decided she'd better see if the dishes were done. As she walked down the darkened hallway she could hear her parents talking quietly in the kitchen.

"It's too bad your Aunt Dorothy is sick, Kate."

"Yes, it must be serious for Lydia to write me from England about it. I guess there's nothing anybody can do except pray that she recovers."

"What about your brother, Henry? What did he have to say?"

"He says he may be able to get me some work on the CPR railway with him this winter."

"Would you be helping him with carpentry work?"

"I don't know. I guess he'll let me know by Christmas. They want to do some work on some of the coaches in January."

"A winter in Winnipeg would be different than on the farm, Billy."

"Well, I guess we'll have to wait and see. I hate to leave you but you'll have Grandpa here if you need him. We sure could use the money. Those taxes are due by summer."

They were sitting at their large wooden pine table in the kitchen. It was clean and the pile of dirty dishes had been washed and dried. Mom's tired head rested on her hand, elbow on the table. Her hands were reddened from the harsh soap and hot water the dishes and the separator were washed in. Shining on her third finger was a single band of gold, the only adornment she was wearing. Growing within her was new life now visible as a small bulge in her loose dress. She was wearing a hand-knit woolen cardigan buttoned only at the top, to allow for her expanding waistline, woolen stockings and flat sensible shoes. Her pretty round face was youthful except for the worried frown over her eyes. Just as Dad reached to give Mom's hand a squeeze he looked up and spotted Ellen as she came into the kitchen.

"Ellen, where've you been? Your mom had to do the dishes herself," scolded Dad.

"Sorry," said Ellen.

"Daisy helped to dry them," said Mom wearily.

"Now, Ellen, you need to help your mother more, especially now that a baby sister or brother is on the way."

"Sorry," said Ellen again. "Could I use the lamp to do some reading?"

"Just don't stay up all night," said Mom.

Ellen picked up the coal oil lamp, scooted down the hallway, and started up the narrow stairs to the bedroom that she shared with her sister Daisy. She held the lamp high, and its motion as she moved, cast pockets of cheerful golden light and purple shadows that danced on the wall lining the stairwell. She stopped at the bookcase in the upstairs hallway, and holding the lamp so she could see, she explored the titles. She soon selected one of her favourite books to read, *The World at Large.*

Her bedroom, as she knew it would be, was cozy with warmth radiating from the bricks that lined the tall chimney stretching up through the center of the house.

Ellen put the lamp on the night table and turned the silver knob controlling the wick in the lantern, its metal feeling rough on her hand. The golden crown of light broadened and brightened the room around her. Her hands were smooth and transparent, haloed in the expanding light. In contrast to the dark shadows behind, her face appeared luminous and delicate with the patterns of light and shadows that played around her head.

She curled up on her bed and opened her book. Like magic, it separated automatically to the page she had last been reading. The navy blue cover on the book was well worn on the corners. Its spine had been reinforced with binding tape. It was one of her mom's textbooks; she had used it when she taught school years ago and it still retained the stale smell of aging chemicals in the paper.

On the two pages that had opened were shiny pictures of a rain forest in British Columbia, another picture of a city street with street cars and large stores and pedestrians walking. There was also a photograph of a beautiful blue lake lined with gold and green trees.

I'm going to visit there one day she thought.

The hum of the lantern blended with the muted conversations downstairs. She read until her eyes became heavy and her mind was full of faraway places. Daisy lightly tiptoed upstairs.

"Haven't you finished reading yet, Ellen?"

"Yeah, I'm ready for bed."

"Wait a minute. Don't turn the light out yet."

Daisy ran downstairs again and picked up her doll, Molly. Holding her tightly, she went back upstairs to her warm bedroom.

"There's no room for a doll in our bed."

"She's not a doll; she's Molly. There's lots of room."

"Oh, all right then. Hurry up so I can put the light out."

After pulling their white nightgowns over their heads and turning the lantern out, the two of them snuggled up in bed, with Molly tucked securely between them. Tomorrow was Saturday and they could sleep in a little instead of heading out in the cold air to school.

Hunting season was in full swing and the white tail deer were plump and plentiful, growing fat on the fields of grain throughout the prairies. Their hides would be thick with fur to survive the cold and insulated with a layer of fat around their bellies. Dad decided that he would try his luck on Saturday morning. Normally he travelled by snowshoe but on this day he thought he would take Nell out hunting instead. She had never been hunting before, but he thought she would help to make the hunt a little easier. He was up early, had a hearty breakfast of crushed wheat and cream and dressed in his white hunting overcoat, pants and warm hat.

He then went out in the icy blue white world to the barn. His footsteps crunched the frozen grass and his exhaled breath formed rings of clouds as he looked at the quiet hazy rose dawn and thought that it would be cold but clear today. At least the wind died down a bit lessening the chill factor.

The barn door creaked open when he lifted the latch. Even the hinges were frozen. Dad was greeted by the animal smells inside the barn. He watched as Nell slowly chewed on some oats that he gave her and noisily drank from the bucket of water. Then he spoke gently to her, explaining where they were going and what hunting would be like. He told her how much she would enjoy riding and tracking deer while he put the saddle on her. He pulled the smooth leather strap through and tightened it up. Nell stopped chewing and stared at Dad with eyes that were dark pools of suspicion as she studied his movements. Her ears twitched back and forth, seeming to question the conversation. This was Saturday and the children were not going to school today. She grunted and nodded her head up and down in response to this change from their normal routine.

While Dad gathered up his gear, his hunting knife and his rifle, he thought: It won't be hard to follow the tracks in the snow. Calvin Stuart shot a four point last week not far from his farm.

Then he went in the back door of the farmhouse and said,

"I'll be back before dinner, Kate. I'm going to take Nell and see what I can find further north."

"Are you sure you want to take Nell?"

"Ah, she's fine. I'm not worried about that."

"Are you going towards the Stuart farm?"

"Yeah, I'll see what tracks there are that way. Tell Grandpa and William to keep that fire burning. It's mighty cold out today."

Mom watched through the frosted glass in the kitchen window as Dad waved, then pulled his woolen toque down over his face so that only his eyes were showing. Dad was almost invisible mounted on Nell and they disappeared down the road and over the hill.

Upstairs, Ellen left the soft warm niche in her bed and went to the window. She drew a circle in the frosted pane of glass, then breathed some warm air on the cold surface and wiped it, clearing enough to see her dad leaving on Nell.

They enjoyed their ride in the crisp silent air.

Dad had time to reflect and ponder the year's challenges, considering what lay ahead and what he could do to resolve their difficulties. The property taxes had to be paid by this summer or they could face the possibility of their farm being put up for auction. He was sure that if he could work with his brother, Henry, this winter in Winnipeg he could earn the badly needed money. His thoughts were interrupted when a large white-tailed buck came into view, just off to his right in a pale frozen field. It was perfect. He and Nell were downwind from it.

"Whoa," he said softly and pulled on the reins.

For a moment the grey brown deer crowned with its symmetrical frost tipped antlers just looked at him. Its shiny dark eyes were emphasized with white rings around them. Large sensitive ears perked up on its strong face and white beard. A shock of white spread down from under its tail and down the buttocks. The hindquarters were solid and muscular.

Dad, slowly and quietly as he could manage, pulled his 30 30 Winchester out of its holster while quietly talking to Nell.

"Easy now girl. Just one more moment. This one's a beauty!"

He pushed the safety ahead, raised the rifle, aimed at the deer, and then squeezed the trigger.

BOOM!

At home in the barn the gentle brown suede cows slowly chewed their hay while Grandpa squeezed their pink teats, and the musical sounds of the squirting warm milk resonated when the milk hit the metal bucket. His legs were long and cramped when he sat on the wooden stool beside the cow. When he was finished he stood up and stretched. His hands were warmed but tired from the work. In the last stall the cow, relieved of her milk, spewed out dark excrement and its odour mixed with those of the hay and sweet milk. William helped Grandpa bring the pails of milk into the kitchen after milking the cows.

It was Mom's job to separate the milk from the cream using a large metal separator that stood in a corner of the kitchen. Usually Ellen helped her, but this morning Ellen was sulking around upstairs, delaying her chores for as long as she could. Her mind was still on wandering across the country and dreaming of adventures she might be lucky enough to experience as soon as she was old enough. Mom poured the foaming milk into the large bowl of the metal separator. Its silver gleamed in the light but was cold to touch. She turned the handle of the machine and watched the milk come out of one spout and cream come out of the other one. The separator was a source of pride to Mom and she was always pleased when her cheque came back with a note stating that the cream was grade A quality.

The milk was kept cool to drink and the thick cream was bottled to send to Winnipeg on the train. It went to a creamery at Eaton's where it was processed into butter and shipped to various cities in the country.

Hot water boiled on the wood stove and when the separating was finished, Mom washed and scalded the separator with boiling hot water. Then she threw a clean towel over it until after dinner when the cows were milked, and the separating had to be done again.

They were all finished with the morning chores. The cattle and horses were fed and watered, chickens were fed and the eggs were gathered and Mom was busy getting their noon day meal of stew and fresh bread ready. The kitchen door opened suddenly and there stood Dad.

"You're home early. Did you get anything?'

Dad's face was red and he walked in with an unmistakable limp.

"That damned fool horse."

"Now, Billy. There's to be no cussing in our house. You mind your language!"

Dad heaved a sigh, and with a little moan found a chair to sit down on.

"Did you hurt yourself?"

"Yeah, and I missed the deer too. Beautiful buck. He was just standing there looking at me. Blast! I had a perfect shot too."

"Now how did you manage to miss it? You never miss."

"That damned fool horse did it."

"What did Nell do?" Ellen asked as she entered the kitchen.

"Threw me right off her back when the gun went off."

"Nell doesn't like guns."

"I thought maybe she's getting older now but there's a little bit of a stubborn devil in her."

"Don't say that, Dad. She's just not used to hunting and guns."

Mom sat down on another chair at the table. She was trying to stay serious while a giggle was rising up in her throat.

"What happened? You're limping. Did you hurt your back?"

"I hit a snow bank full on. My whole body is sore."

"Did Nell stay with you or did you have to walk home?"

Mom's shoulders shook with suppressing the laughter.

"No, she didn't go far. She came back and just stood there looking at me."

"Well, since you're home, we might as well have dinner. Ellen, go find Grandpa and William. I think Daisy's in the parlour."

Mom then got busy setting the table with their hot dinner while Dad, still grumbling, pulled off his boots, took off his jacket and got ready to eat with his family.

The school children worked hard all day Monday to finish up the last of the schoolwork for this term and make Christmas decorations for the hall next door. They piled into the community hall beside the schoolhouse after school, and Miss Larson lined them up in two rows to practice their songs for Friday's Christmas pageant.

Miss Larson said,

"There, Ellen. You stand beside George since you two are the tallest. William, stand beside Mary and then Mabel. James, over here, beside Mabel. There, that's right. Now in the front row, Joy and Sarah, then Joseph and Raymond. Daisy, stand there beside Raymond and Helen, you stand here on the end. Remember your places on Friday night."

Ellen scrunched up her shoulders and tried not to get too close to George. She frowned at him as if to say, "Keep your distance!"

Annoyed, George snickered, and halfway through *"Silent Night"* he leaned into Ellen and whispered, "Freckle face! Freckle face!"

At that Ellen quickly picked up her foot and stomped on his as hard as she could. He recoiled with pain, squinting his eyes and bracing his teeth. Her lips curled up in a smug smile and her eyes gleamed with satisfaction. Revenge was sweet!

"All eyes should be up front on me," Miss Larson said.

"Okay, that's good. Tomorrow we'll finish putting up the decorations that you've made and then I think we'll be all ready. Class dismissed. See you tomorrow."

Friday night came and after all of the preparations and practicing they were ready and eager to join their neighbours for the Christmas pageant that the school children had rehearsed for. They set off in the cold still night snug inside the sleigh box pulled by Nell and her partner, Sal, towards the community hall. Earlier, Dad had filled the sleigh with fresh hay, then covered it with warm blankets. Once inside they were comfortable with wool blankets over their knees, their bodies close together, keeping them warm as they sped along.

Grandpa rubbed his beard as he thought of his bag that he'd snuck behind them under the hay in the sleigh. He loved his annual job at the school pageant.

"Dad, look at the sky!" exclaimed Ellen.

"Whoa," said Dad. "Let's have a better look."

"The stars are on fire!" said William.

Mom's face lit up in admiration of the spectacular show of lime green and yellow white lights that were streaking and dancing across the sky. It was as if an artist's paintbrush was excitedly moving swirls of flowing color through the dark atmosphere.

"It looks like angels are tiptoeing across the sky," said Daisy.

"Maybe your Grandma is one of the angels," said Grandpa.

They all watched spellbound as the shocks of light brightened up the dark winter sky. The pinnacles of animated light that streamed to the heavens left a filmy tail behind them.

"Those are northern lights," said Dad.

"I think the correct name for them is aurora borealis," said Mom.

"How'd they get there?" said William.

"I don't know, William, but they certainly are exciting to see," said Mom.

"Thanks for stopping, Billy. This is a sight I might not see again," said Grandpa.

"Sure you will, Grandpa," said Mom.

"I still think angels are making the lights," said Daisy.

"Maybe you're right," said Mom.

They resumed their journey through the flashing night.

Inside, the community hall was dressed in its Christmas finest. There were large winter paintings arranged on the walls, strings of paper chains looped between them. Paper bells and holly had been coloured, cut out, and strung up at the front of the stage. A Christmas tree, decorated with homemade cards and popcorn balls hanging from it, was proudly displayed in the left corner of the hall. At the top of the tree was a large shiny star made with silver paper. On the stage there was a background for a nativity scene set up with bales of hay and a wooden manger. Around the edges of the hall, the lights from the lamps against the darkness created a magical indoors starry night.

Ellen held her breath when she saw it all. It was magic. Christmas magic!

CHAPTER 5
THE CHRISTMAS HOLIDAYS

Ellen found her seat in the front row with the rest of her class and sat down. The rhythmic flow of low chatter and familiar greetings rose and echoed through the hall and into the still starry night outdoors.

A faint trace of lilacs floated in the air around Miss Larson. She looked radiant in the subtle lighting, her strawberry blonde hair rolled up in a chignon sparkled gold with hints of crimson. Ellen's eyes lit up with admiration as she gazed at Miss Larson. Her well-fitted dress was highlighted with buttons that marched like soldiers down her back and perfectly matched the colour of her dress and the narrow belt around her waist. Miss Larson was wearing a stylish store bought dress unlike the homemade clothes her students wore.

Ellen's mind wandered as she twirled one of her dark silky curls through her fingers.

I wonder if I'll ever look that pretty. I'm so skinny, she thought.

Her attention drifted back to only two nights before. In her bedroom she had gazed at her boyish stick like figure in the faithful mirror looking back at her. Her youthful but awkward form was still innocent, a flower not yet blooming. Curious about what she would look like with breasts, she stuffed a pair of leggings under her blouse. Then she cocked to one side and placed her hands on her hips and looked at the reformed body in the mirror.

"What are you doing?" said Daisy.

Ellen jumped, and turning to one side quickly, removed the leggings.

"None of your business," answered Ellen.

"Mom says she needs help downstairs. Better hurry up."

"Ellen, Ellen," called a voice in the distance.

Ellen was jerked back to the present when a firmer voice addressed her again.

"Ellen, Ellen!" the voice said louder. "Can you move your chair a bit?"

Ellen's memory drifted away like the morning mist, and with a sigh she thought, I don't think I'll ever look like that.

Miss Larson cast a worried look at the piano then back again at the door.

She should be here by now, she thought. I hope nothing's wrong.

Miss Larson checked her watch. It was time to start. Everyone except Mrs. Saunders was there. With a look of unease, Miss Larson spoke to Mary's mother, Mrs. Gordon,

"Where's Mrs. Saunders?"

"I'm not sure. Perhaps you should ask Mrs. Stuart."

"Miss Larson, Mrs. Saunders asked me to send you a message," Jenny Stuart interrupted.

"She's come down with the flu, and she says she's sorry but she just can't come tonight. She's got a high fever and is feeling very unwell. She hopes you and the children can manage without her."

Miss Larson was quiet for a moment, then said,

"Influenza! Well of course if she's sick it's better for her to stay at home. I hope she's feeling better soon."

Miss Larson looked over at the lonely piano bench and thought, Oh dear, I wonder how the children will sound without the piano. I guess we'll just have to make do without her.

While chairs were still scraping and conversations were humming, Miss Larson went to the front row to talk to the children.

"We don't have Mrs. Saunders to play the piano for us, so you'll have to sing your very best without her."

"How about if I play the piano for the class?" said a familiar voice from behind Ellen.

Ellen turned to see her mother slowly rising from her seat behind her. Ellen's cheeks turned a self conscious pink and she cast her eyes down and looked the other way. Her mother was going to play music in front of everyone! Oh, no. I'm so embarrassed she thought.

"If you can, we'd really appreciate it," said Miss Larson. "The music is on the piano."

"It's been a while since I've played, but I'll have a look at it. I'm sure I won't have any trouble," said Mom.

"Thank you, Mrs. Graham. The piano is right over here," said Miss Larson with a relieved sigh.

Mom went over to the piano. She ran her fingers across the shiny wood and the lustrous white and black keys, and sat down. She spent a few minutes looking over the sheet music, then started to play *"The First Noel"* one of the Christmas carols Miss Larson laid out on the piano. The children and guests stopped talking and listened to the confident and lyrical music. Mom was transformed. Her face relaxed into a happy grin as she embraced the keyboard. Ellen perked up. She was aware that her mom knew how to play the piano, but she didn't know that she could play so well. This was a side of her mom that she wasn't familiar with. Her discomfort eased into awakened pride and Ellen smiled as she got lost in the music.

Daisy came to life portraying Mary in the recreation of the Christmas story. Molly did her part as the baby Jesus and James was Joseph. Daisy was a gentle spirit, and the role seemed to suit her kind and loving instincts. Small and frail, she seemed to almost disappear into her costume made from worn out sheets.

Then it was William's turn. He stood proud and tall, then cleared his throat while the audience respectfully settled into quiet anticipation. He cleared his throat again, then looked over at Grandpa who was smiling at him. William's voice was shaky, coming through small and a little croaky as he started,

"Twas the night before Christmas."

He hesitated, looking a little frightened. Then once more he glanced at Grandpa who winked at him and nodded. William cleared his throat again with determination and with a much louder voice he continued,

"and all through the house."

His poem gained momentum while his voice gathered strength and enthusiasm. By the time he was finished his recitation, he was smiling with satisfaction at the drama he had been able to throw into the poem. The audience's loud applause thundered through the hall, surrounding William with warm approval.

The children filled their assigned places at the front of the hall to perform the Christmas carols they had worked so hard at. The audience felt a stirring of emotion as they joined in to sing, *"Silent Night."* The sweet melodic sounds soaked the air, saturated it, then, swelling, they overflowed into their clear cold silent night outdoors. When Ellen looked back at the audience she smiled inwardly. Grandpa was not in his chair.

"Ho, Ho, Ho! Merry Christmas everyone!"

The younger children gasped in excitement. It was Santa Claus! He'd come to their concert. Santa came trotting through the door and into the hall, down the side and up to the front where a chair was waiting for him. He put down his sack and, with a twinkle in his eyes, said to Miss Larson,

"Have these children been well behaved all year? Have they been doing their homework?"

Miss Larson replied that they had and the children smiled in relief.

"Well then, let them come up and see what I have for them," said Santa.

The school children lined up with the youngest ones at the beginning of the line. The audience chuckled in approval as each child sat on Santa's knee and shyly answered his questions.

"What would you like for Christmas?" said Santa.

"I'd like a new wagon," said Raymond.

"A big wagon, or a little wagon?"

"A little one."

"What about your brother, does he want a wagon too?"

"No, he wants a tin of toy soldiers."

"What will you do with your wagon?"

"Help my dad with the haying."

"I'll have to see what I can do on Christmas Eve."

Mom turned to watch Santa from her piano seat. She thought to herself, he seems to be getting thinner. I had to take in his pants at the waist at least an inch this year.

With a red sticky mouth and waving a creamy melted half-eaten candy cane in his hand, William joined the other children in saying goodbye to Santa. The candies he received were even better than last year's. William was sure of that because he sampled them right away.

The long frozen night opened its arms wide to welcome the families back to the comfort of their homes. The concert was over for another year and the children could celebrate a whole month of holidays before returning to school for another term.

Just before dusk the next day, Mom was about to announce that their evening meal was ready. Grandpa was looking out of the kitchen window when he spotted Dad snowshoeing towards home. His grey silhouette was fuzzy in the dimming light. He was carrying a lifeless buck wrapped around his neck and braced on his shoulders. With his gun in one hand and the heavy load on his back he plodded towards home. Grandpa's eyes twinkled and he smiled at the sight of Billy carrying that large deer.

"Come and have a look, Kate."

"Looks like he caught that deer he's been tracking."

"Good sized one, I'd say."

"Yes, I guess we'll have lots of meat through the winter."

"Are you going to can some venison, Kate?"

"Oh, I probably will. Makes good stew."

"Is there room in the freezer box for some venison?"

"The box on the roof was full of frozen meat on Thanksgiving, but I think we can find room for some more."

Grandpa smiled and added, "Once we take our Christmas turkey out there'll be lots of room up there. I'm looking forward to that turkey dinner. You know, Grandma used to make the best gravy.

So do you, Kate. I especially like it poured over the mashed potatoes and the turkey meat. And plum pudding for dessert! Are you going to make a pudding this year?"

"Don't worry, Grandpa. It's all been made and just waiting for you."

Grandpa gave Kate a little hug as he passed her on the way to the back door.

"Tell Billy that dinner's ready. Ellen, go find Daisy and William. It's time to eat."

Dad joined them for dinner, and later he went out to the barn with William and Grandpa. They helped him skin and hang the deer. Ellen didn't like to look at the blank eyes in the deer's head, or the blood red carcass left hanging from its hind feet from a wooden beam in the barn before being cut up and preserved, so she stayed in the kitchen with Mom and Daisy.

In the morning, it was Ellen's job to clean the oil lamps. The glass was sullied with veiled coal like shades of purple and black. She had to take a ball attached to a stick, wrap a rag around it and scrub the sooty grime from the cooled inner surface of the glass chimneys on the lamps. It was not her favourite job and she had trouble containing her grumbles as she worked to bring the lamps back to a restored shiny and energetic glow. She ran her blackened fingers over an old towel hanging from a hook in the kitchen, heaved a sigh, and stepped back to inspect the newly transparent glass.

Dad came into the kitchen carrying his collected bundle of hides. He was softly whistling to himself as he sorted out pelts from weasels, wolves, muskrats and beaver. Ellen put the lamps aside, and amazed that anything could be that soft and sleek, she sunk her hands into the luxuriously soft silky warmth. The ends of the fur tickled her skin as she brushed it against her cheek. Dad placed them carefully over the backs of the kitchen chairs and counted them.

"Have you got enough furs to take to Winnipeg, Billy?" Mom asked.

"Yup. I think it's time to go. I'd like to get them sold before Christmas. I need to talk to Henry about some work too. The deer will be all right in the barn until I get back."

The smell of the hides rose up and mixed with the yeasty smell of rising bread dough. Mom took the towel off of the large ceramic bowl where the growing mound was expanding. With a hiss the dough sank in the center when Mom punched it down, covered it, and allowed it to rest for a few minutes before shaping it into loaves of bread.

"How are the prices at Soudak's this year?"

"Not sure. Hopefully, they're paying a good price. We can sure use the money."

"If I hurry I can make the evening train. Can you pack me a lunch, Kate?"

"Sure, I have some leftover roast to make sandwiches with."

With his furs in a pack slung over his back and a sack with his lunch in it and wearing snowshoes, Dad headed out into the crisp sharp air. As Ellen watched through the frosty window, the roadway rose up to meet his firm footsteps towards Pratt and the railway station where he would find the ride to Winnipeg.

The Graham family was absorbed with Christmas preparations. Grandpa and William cut down a tree to decorate with paper chains and homemade baubles while Mom checked the traditional plum pudding, and as the winter solstice approached, the farmhouse prepared to celebrate the Christmas festival and the earth's continuing journey towards the rebirth of spring. Its warmth was a barrier to the cold landscape lit up by a low hanging gold and orange sun in the sky by day, and long inky darkness with soft sparkling hills at night.

Chapter 6
Winter Chills

"Hurry up, Ellen. My arms are getting tired," said William.

"Just hold still till I get this wool wound up," Ellen replied.

Ellen's sleek smooth hands fumbled with the soft grey and white tweed wool as she pulled the stitches out row by row and wound the kinky worn wool around William's waiting arms. The ticklish strands of wool that slid through her hands felt scratchy against the pale skin on his arms. Ellen was concentrating; her eyes held a distant opaque look as she was recycling the wool from an old sweater by ripping out the stitches. She planned to knit the fuzzy grey wool into a scarf. Last night her mom showed her how to hold the needles, and Ellen awkwardly practiced moving the needles between her fingers and winding the wool around to create the stocking stitch, plain stitches on the first row, and purled stitched on the next.

"How long is Dad going to be away?" Daisy asked from the rocking chair.

"I don't know. He's working with Uncle Henry," Ellen answered.

"Is it far away?" Daisy asked.

"I guess so. I hope he comes home soon."

Daisy climbed down from the big rocking chair and placed Molly into her cradle. Then she started to set up her new little china teapot and teacups that Santa had brought her for Christmas. The sunlight from the window sparkled on the creamy white and pink flowered tea set that Daisy now pretended to pour tea from.

Daisy covered Molly with a new little pink blanket that Mom had made for her for Christmas, smoothed her doll's woolen curls on her head, and then climbed back up into the large wooden rocker. Her small delicate arms straddled the smooth arms of the chair. Pools of cold January sunlight filtered through the small parlour window caressing the three children while they played.

William's arms sank lower with each passing of the wool and his eyelids slowly started to droop over his blue eyes. His eyelashes fluttered, wanting to shut out the world from his sleepy reddened eyes, and small damp strands of golden hair clung to his forehead.

His cheeks were flushed and his heavy head found refuge on the arm of the couch. His energy was disappearing, evaporating from his limp body. His chest began to rise and fall with short shallow breaths.

"What's the matter, William?" said Ellen.

She put down her wool and took a better look at her brother. She poked him in the arm but William just shrugged her off and closed his eyes again.

"Mom, I think you should have a look at William. He doesn't look too good."

Mom was passing through the hallway and she stopped and came to look at him.

"What's wrong, William?"

"I'm just tired, Mom. My throat is a bit sore."

His eyes squinted at the offensive sunlight.

Mom felt his forehead with her hand, and with both of her cool hands cupped his flushed cheeks. He had a fever. She peered at him for a moment, quietly assessing his symptoms. A worried crease formed over her eyes and her face became thoughtful.

"I think you should be in bed," Mom said.

"But it's still daytime," moaned William.

"Never mind, you'll feel better with some rest. Come on, up you get. We're going upstairs to bed. I want to check to see if you have a rash."

"You two stay down here," Mom said to Ellen and Daisy.

William stood up on the colourful braided rug that graced the wooden floors in the parlour. The wool trousers he was wearing felt like a burning furnace next to his tender hot skin. Mom reached under his arm and held him steady while they both took feeble steps towards the hallway.

The blood seemed to rush from his head to his feet. His head pounded with driving pain while he focused on a patch of blue cone flowers on the wall-paper. The flowers blurred and danced around and around, spinning towards William and Mom.

"Here, let me help him," said Grandpa and he wrapped one strong arm under William's arms and guided him up the groaning stairs. Mom followed close behind while Ellen watched their ascent from the parlour doorway. Daisy dropped from the wooden rocking chair beside the sofa, letting the squeaking rocker break the searching silence in the air.

"What's wrong with William?" asked Daisy.

"I don't know," said Ellen, putting her ball of wool down.

"Maybe he caught a cold when we were playing outside. Mom told him to wear his long warm underwear."

"I think he did."

"But he gave me his mittens, because mine were wet and my hands were cold. Do you think that was what made him sick?"

"No, we weren't out there for very long and we got warmed up by the fire in the wood stove in the kitchen when we came in."

"Don't worry, Daisy. I'm sure he'll be fine. He probably ate too much or something."

Ellen wasn't as reassured as she tried to make Daisy feel though. She knew that there was a disease called influenza going around their area. Last night, she had listened at the doorway when Mom and Grandpa were talking. They didn't know she was there. In fact, she knew she would be in trouble for "eavesdropping," as her Mom would say. Ellen was always interested in adult conversations. How else would she know what was going on? This one was a bit troubling as she recalled what was said.

"Mrs. Saunders was very ill. They nearly lost her," Mom said.

"Mr. Peterson at the General Store said that the doctor was very busy with calls to sick families. He said that some whole families were sick and there was no one to look after them. Mr. Peterson says that the flu is spreading like wildfire. He says that the little one at the Reid farm is in very serious condition," Mom continued.

Lost in her ponderings, Ellen's shoulders tensed and she stumbled with her knitting when she thought about the worried look that had passed between Mom and Grandpa, and remembered the disturbing conversation she'd heard about the flu spreading throughout their community, leaving a trail of sick people behind.

I wonder if William has influenza. I hope he'll be all right, she thought. What happens if you get influenza? What do you do about it came the silent questions that dashed through her mind.

She tried hard to remember what Mom had said. I think she said that Mrs. Saunders was recovering. Her thoughts continued to race with questions, until they were interrupted by Daisy.

"What does contagious mean?"

"Where did you hear that?" asked Ellen.

"I heard it from listening to Mom talking. She said that some people were getting sick and that it was contagious."

"It means that anyone can get sick from someone else who is sick."

"You mean we could get sick too, Ellen?"

"Don't worry about it, Daisy. William will be okay."

"I don't want Molly to get sick."

"She won't. Now grab that wool and let's finish unraveling it. Here, that's right."

Ellen's mind refused to be still, racing with unanswered questions. She put down the ball of wool she was winding when she suddenly remembered Mom's thick worn medical book stored in the upstairs bookshelf. It was only last week, when she was curious about the differences between boys and girls, she secretly looked at the chapters in the book that would give her that information. These were things that she couldn't ask her mom about, but the long words that she tried to figure out were still a mystery. Now she needed to know what influenza was and what would happen if they got it. She had an idea that the book might tell her what she wanted to know.

"Where are you going? Mom said to stay here," said Daisy.

"I'll be right back. You stay here."

Ellen quietly ascended the tall stairs up to their bedrooms. She crept past the doorway to William's bedroom. Mom was busy undressing William while Grandpa was watching them. Nobody saw her sneak by.

There it is she thought as her fingers slid down the blue cover of the book she was looking for. It was old and well worn, hidden in between *Grimm's Fairytales* and *Peter Pan*. It's importance was elevated by the sheer weight of it.

Ellen found a spot under her bedroom window and ran her finger down the index. She turned to Chapter 5, Communicable Diseases, and looked for the word influenza. When she found it she started to read. She was silent for a few minutes and her eyes narrowed into a worried frown.

It is contagious she thought as she read the stern looking text. He does have the same symptoms. At least I think he does. I hope I don't get it. Well, I can't worry Daisy about it. She closed her eyes while thinking about what she had just read. Oh William, please be all right.

"What are you reading?" asked Daisy.

Ellen jumped and closed the old book with a bang and then put it behind her, away from Daisy's reach. Her mom's voice caught her attention.

"Grandpa, he's burning up with fever!"

"I know what to get. I'll be right back," said Grandpa.

Ellen peeked into William's bedroom and Daisy was trying to catch a glimpse from behind her. William was in bed with his patchwork quilt snugly tucked in. His woolen trousers were hanging from their suspenders on the bedpost. His face was flushed and sweaty, and his reddened eyes were closed. Soon Grandpa came in from behind Ellen with a wooden bucket of cool snow and Mom began packing a clean striped towel with the frozen snow. Then she laid it against William's flushed face and neck.

Ellen couldn't help but stare at William's glossy red cheeks and sweaty young body that peeked out from beneath the quilt.

"Here, let's take this quilt off and just leave a sheet. He's too warm for that heavy thing."

Mom quickly removed the quilt and laid it in a corner of the room. William's body was limp and listless under the thin cotton cover Mom left on him.

"Can I do anything to help?" said Ellen.

"Oh, Ellen. You shouldn't be here. And neither should you, Daisy," Mom said hurriedly while she was trying to make William more comfortable.

"Check our dinner on the stove, Ellen, and keep Daisy downstairs and away from William. Now off you go."

"Come on, Daisy. We need to be downstairs," said Ellen and she quickly ushered Daisy and Molly down the whimpering stairs and back to the empty still parlour.

Ellen followed the smell of simmering vegetable soup in the kitchen. She hurried as she rounded the corner into the small kitchen. The soup was boiling hard and spitting out from beneath the heavy metal lid that covered it. She grabbed the lid to prevent it from boiling over on to the stove and immediately let it go, the lid landing on the floor with a loud clanging sound.

"Yikes!" she yelled as the heat scorched her fingers.

"Here, this might help," said Grandpa, as he passed her with his bucket of snow.

"Use this to cool your hand."

Grandpa held the bucket out to Ellen and she held her burning fingers in the cold icy slush. Once she caught her breath, she picked up the rebellious lid with a towel, turned the damper down and sunk into a kitchen chair. The perplexing problem of William's illness crowded her mind and was written on her frowning face.

"Grandpa, what's influenza?" asked Ellen.

"Oh, it's nothing you need to worry about. William will be right as rain very soon. It just has to run its course."

"Will I get it?"

"I hope not."

"But, Grandpa. It's contagious."

"Don't worry about that," said Grandpa, a little more impatiently than she was used to.

Later when Mom, Grandpa, Ellen and Daisy sat down to dinner they ate in silence. Mom tried to look happy but worried creases would not leave her forehead.

Ellen and Daisy went to bed early that night.

Ellen slept fitfully, interrupted several times by the sound of footsteps on the stairs and Mom returning to William's room throughout the night.

Even before the morning light peered in through her window, Ellen woke up feeling an uncomfortable warmth in her and Daisy's bed. She stirred, then kicked off the blankets before realizing that the warmth she was feeling was Daisy beside her. Her small body was limp and sweaty and she was murmuring softly.

"Daisy, what's wrong. Are you okay?"

Daisy didn't answer her. Ellen felt her and was startled when she realized that Daisy was burning with fever.

"Daisy, answer me. Are you okay?"

She half raised her eyelids and said,

"My head hurts and so does my throat."

Ellen moved quickly. She had to find Mom. She had to tell her that Daisy was sick too. The cold floor and the cool air was a sharp contrast to her bed with an overheated body next to her. Ellen hurried to her parents' bedroom but no one was there. The bed was still made and the covers that were carefully folded had only a slight crease where Mom must have laid down for a few brief rests.

"Mom, where are you?" Ellen called.

On her way back through the hallway she stopped and looked in William's room.

"Mom, are you there?"

She heard a stirring, then saw her mom sitting on a chair beside William's bed. Her bent head was resting on the wall beside her and her hands were protectively wrapped around the abundant bulge in her midsection. She was still wearing yesterday's dress, worn and wrinkled, and partly unbuttoned revealing glistening warm skin. Damp spots of sweat lay in patches on the bodice of her dress and there was the unmistakable stale smell of vomit floating in William's room. Ellen realized that her mom hadn't gone to bed last night because she had been so busy looking after William. William was still sleeping but he looked a little more peaceful to Ellen.

"Ellen, come here," she heard her mom whisper.

"Mom, what's wrong?"

Ellen looked fearfully at her Mom's tired and sweaty face.

"I don't feel good," said Mom. "Listen to me. We need help. You need to get Grandpa."

"Mom, are you sick too?" said Ellen.

"I'm afraid so. Go and get Grandpa."

Ellen, still in her nightgown and in bare feet, sprinted down the stairs to find her grandpa in his room by the kitchen. She didn't have to wake him. Grandpa was already getting up from his bed. While sitting on the edge of his bed he listened as Ellen told him about Mom and Daisy. His face dissolved into a sea of worried lines and his shoulders stooped a little lower. Grandpa stood up and with a snap of the elastic in his suspenders he pulled them over his shoulders, his pants rising up and covering the long white underwear he was wearing.

"Okay, Ellen. I'm coming."

Upstairs again, Ellen tried to make Daisy more comfortable. She picked up Molly and tucked her beside Daisy. Then she took off the quilt and straightened a sheet on top of her. Ellen's heart was racing. It was what she feared. Her family was all sick with influenza.

Grandpa helped Mom into bed and then with a deep sigh and a long look at Mom, he said to Ellen,

"We need help, Ellen. We need to send a telegram to your Dad to come home. I don't know if the doctor is available but we need his help too."

"Mom is really sick, isn't she, Grandpa?"

"Yes, William and Daisy too."

"They'll get better, won't they Grandpa?"

"We'll do our best."

"We can send a telegram from the store in Pratt," said Ellen.

"Yes, said Grandpa softly as he looked from one bedroom doorway to the other.

"I can do it," said Ellen. "I'm not sick and Nell can take me there."

"It's very cold, Ellen. Are you sure you can make the ride?"

"I can do it, Grandpa. Nell and I. We can do it. Nell will take me. I'll be all right."

"Okay, Ellen," said Grandpa wearily. "You'd better dress warm. I'll help you saddle Nell and get her ready."

Quickly and mindlessly, Ellen got dressed, ran downstairs and grabbed a piece of bread from the kitchen shelf to eat on her way outdoors. She knew she had to hurry. There was no time to do the morning chores but maybe Grandpa would look after the animals while she was gone.

The crisp cold unforgiving air was a shock to her, biting the skin on her face. She pulled a scarf up around her mouth and her toque down covering to the top of her eyes. The awakening morning was grey and ashen, but she was too intent on her journey to acknowledge it. She didn't pay attention to the crunching her boots made on the frosted snowy ground or to the tingling in her throat and the difficulty swallowing the bread she brought with her. Her head was bent and she didn't notice how stark the barn looked as she passed through it. Her only thought was to get to Pratt to send a telegram to her dad and to find Dr. Albertson.

"We need to hurry, Nell. You need to take me to Pratt. There's a girl, Nell. We'll make it, you'll see," said Ellen, as she gave Nell a quick pat on her neck while offering her some oats in a small bucket alternating with some water.

Nell's chewing ceased momentarily and she gave a snort as she looked at Ellen. The urgency of their mission was acknowledged and reflected in Nell's intelligent eyes.

Grandpa finished putting the saddle on Nell and led her out of the barn.

"It's seven miles in bitter cold, girl. Make sure you ride careful," said Grandpa.

"I will, Grandpa. Don't worry. Nell will take me there and I'll get help."

Ellen glanced backwards as she and Nell were riding away from the farm. Grandpa looked small and stooped, a sad shadow flickering on the misty snow, as he raised his hand in a gesture of goodbye.

Nell was urged on with a flick of the reins. It wasn't the carefree ride she was used to enjoying and they had a long way to go in the cold grey cavern of worry that engulfed them.

The pale grey outline of the general store and the train station took form on the distant prairie as Ellen rode towards it. It was bathed in the early morning feeling, a lonely feeling, just before the new day's warmth spread over the colour drained buildings and the monochromatic landscape. She was spent and hot, even in the bitter cold, and could only see through the pounding pain in her head as she was carried forward by Nell. Her body had drooped lower and lower on Nell but she managed to hang on and keep talking to her.

"Keep going girl. We need to get to the store."

Nell, strong and steady, knew where she was going and she courageously carried Ellen towards Pratt.

As they neared their destination Nell broke into a trot and finally stopped at the store's front stairs. Her knock was answered quickly by Mrs. Peterson who had been busy stocking shelves, a job she liked to do early in the morning before customers arrived.

"It's Ellen Graham!" said Mrs. Peterson, surprised by her early morning visitor.

Ellen was leaning on the door frame, her heavy head seeking somewhere to lean against. The wood frame was freezing cold but a relief to her hot skin. Sweat was dripping down her forehead from under her toque.

"Ellen, what are you doing here? You look sick. Charles, come quick. We need some help here."

Mr. Peterson appeared in the doorway. He took a quick look at Ellen then wrapped his arm under hers and helped her into the warm interior of the store.

Ellen struggled to focus her sore eyes in the indoor light. She sighed, then looked sideways for somewhere to sit down. The tiredness was spreading through her body and she was panting. Hanging on to Mr. Peterson for support, she was housing a raging fire and in a voice that was reduced to a whisper she said, "Mr. Peterson, I have to send a telegram to my father. He's working in Winnipeg and we need him to come home because my family is all sick."

"You look like you're sick too, Ellen," said Mrs. Peterson. "Here child, let me help you with your coat."

Mrs. Peterson guided Ellen to a wooden chair that was sitting by the large wooden barrel under the front window. She shed her coat, then her toque and mittens. Her hair was damp and stuck to her head and her shoulders stooped inside her woolen sweater she was wearing.

"Your family will need the doctor too, I'm guessing," said Mr. Peterson.

Ellen nodded weakly.

"I'll need to know where I'm sending the telegram to."

"It's to William Graham at Cross Street Boarding House in St. Vital, Winnipeg.

"Okay, I've got it. I'll get that done right now. Martha, you take care of Ellen. I'll tend to Ellen's horse as soon as I send the telegram."

As Ellen looked up she was aware of the sharpened colours inside the store. She tried to focus through the pain in her throbbing head but the shelves that were lined with variegated reds, blues, greens and yellows seemed to swirl and dance around her. The psychedelic confusion of rainbow-like colours tumbled and played with her consciousness until they all turned dark, then faded from Ellen's view.

Chapter 7
The Journey Home

Ellen woke intermittently. She was vaguely aware of cold cloths bathing her face and neck, and then the voices. Some of the voices were familiar but some were not. The voices seemed to fade in and out, their words unclear, until sleep overcame her.

At last, Ellen opened her eyes taking in the room around her. She looked from one corner to the other. It wasn't her bedroom. It wasn't even her house. It was a small room. Soft filmy white curtains framed the window and tiny printed pink rosebuds graced the wallpaper on the four walls of the bedroom. There was a large beige and white pitcher and bowl on the dresser across the room. A coal oil lamp sat on a white crocheted doily on the bed table beside her, and an empty kitchen chair was against the wall opposite her. She was tucked in with a handmade puffy quilt. The star pattern, she thought, in the same colours that were on the walls. Surrounding her in the bed was the fragrance of clean white sheets and the sharp crispness of sturdy white cotton that she slid back and forth and turned in. She was dressed in a white cotton nightgown. It wasn't hers. Whose was it? Where was she? What happened? She took a deep breath and her memory slowly returned. Mom, Daisy, were they all right? What about William? She had no idea how much time had passed. Where was everyone?

As she started to remember her ride to the Peterson's, she realized that she must be in their home. Her eyes squinted with the residue headache that was still seated across the top of her head. She started to pull herself out of the bed, then changed her mind and fell back down onto the support of the comfortable soft mattress that squeaked in time with her movements within the brass coloured metal headboard.

She was tired but didn't sleep, and the voices could still be heard. One voice sounded like her dad's. Yes, it was her dad's voice outside her bedroom door. Her dad was here. He came home. Ellen smiled and relaxed in spite of her weakness. Her dad was talking to another man whose voice she didn't recognize. Ellen strained to hear what they were saying but the words seemed to blend into each other.

Ellen watched as the door knob on the bedroom door turned and in walked Dr. Albertson and her dad.

"Ellen, you're awake," said Dad, relief evident on his face.

"How are you feeling?" said Dr. Albertson.

"I'm still a bit tired but I guess I'm okay," said Ellen.

Her dad moved towards her and leaning down he took her hand in his hands. Then he gave her a light kiss on the top of her head. Somehow the blue in his eyes had faded with fatigue and new worry lines appeared on his handsome face.

"Dad, I'm so glad you're back."

"I got the telegram three days ago and came right away."

"Three days! Have I been here that long?"

"Yes, you were a very sick girl. That ride! Oh, Ellen. I'm so glad you're recovering from the flu."

His voice broke and he looked down to hide his watery eyes.

"Mom, Daisy, William. Are they okay?"

"Yes, they're over it. Dr. Albertson saw them. They're all recovering nicely."

"Grandpa. What about Grandpa?"

"He's sick right now, Ellen, but I'm sure he'll be up and well very soon."

"Did anyone look after Nell?"

"Nell is at home. She's fine. Mr. Peterson fed and watered her, then kept her until I arrived."

While they were talking, Dr. Albertson was opening his leather medical bag and removed his stethoscope. The doctor was a middle aged man. His knowing eyes peeked out from under dark eyebrows. His round smiling face was framed by a dark beard. He was short and wearing a brown tweed suit that gave the impression that nothing could go wrong with this kind doctor in charge. He pulled back her quilt while saying, "I'm just going to listen to your heart and lungs, Ellen. I think you're over the worst but we'll just make sure."

Dr. Albertson then slipped the cold round metal part of the stethoscope under her nightgown and held it there first on her upper chest while he listened through the attached tubes that were plugged into his ears. He didn't say a word then moved it further down to either side of her chest and her back where he listened again.

He removed the stethoscope and put it back into his bag. Then he picked up her wrist with one hand, fingers over her pulse, flipped open the lid of his pocket watch and checked her heart rate.

"Sounds good. You'll be back to normal as soon as you get some strength back. She's lucky that she doesn't have any secondary infections, Billy. I think you'll be able to make the trip home now, Ellen."

"I've got the sleigh here," said Dad. "I can take her home today."

Once more, Dr. Albertson took out the gold pocket watch that was in his vest pocket and with a quick glance at the numbers on its face, he said, "Well, I should be going. You're a brave girl, Ellen. Take good care of her Billy."

"Thanks for everything," said Dad as he opened the bedroom door and followed him out.

Their farmhouse sang out a welcome as Ellen and Dad approached it in their sleigh. The gentle familiarity of her home was joyful. Like a favourite blanket, it wrapped her in a feeling of warmth and comfort. Smoke that puffed from its chimney curled up into a clear blue sky that contrasted the white hills and fields surrounding the farmhouse.

Once they were indoors, Ellen inhaled the fragrance of home in the barn smell that clung to her dad's jacket and the wood smoke from the crackling fireplace. She was relieved to see the discarded winter boots and pools of dripping snow on the floor by the door accompanied by a pair of wet mittens distorted by frozen chunks of snow. Things appeared to be back to normal in the farmhouse.

Ellen heard William's voice in the parlour and rounded the corner to see him sitting on the braided rug playing with some shiny glass marbles he'd been given at Christmas. He was still a little pale but had the focused impish look that Ellen was used to seeing on his face.

"Ellen! You're back," he exclaimed. He hurriedly put his marbles down and ran to give his sister a hug. Then his face broke into a smile.

"I thought I'd get your Christmas candies. I know where your stash is," he teased.

Ellen just laughed and embraced him again. She was so glad to be home.

"Where's Daisy?" asked Ellen.

"She's in bed having a nap," answered her dad. "Here let me help you with your coat."

"But she's all right?"

"Yes, Ellen. She's just fine."

Ellen climbed the stairs. She was still tired but she needed to see her mom and Daisy.

"Ellen, is that you?" she heard her mom call as she neared the top of the stairs. Ellen looked inside the doorway. Her mom was sitting up in bed and she held her arms up reaching for Ellen.

"Come here, Ellen."

Her voice faltered, then Mom gathered Ellen into her arms and pressed her tightly in an emotionally charged embrace. Ellen inhaled the scent that was distinctly her mom's and felt the cool crisp cotton of her nightgown. Mom hardly dared to let go as though she wanted to keep Ellen within her reach forever. Mom's eyes were watery and she seemed to be at a loss for words until she finally said,

"Thank God you're home and recovering. We're all okay, even your new little brother here," Mom said as she patted her middle.

"Or sister," said Dad from the doorway of their bedroom.

"Would you like more tea?"

"No, I'm not thirsty," said Mom.

Dad picked up the tray that was leaning against the wall and started to fill it with the teapot and the cup and saucer that was resting on the night table beside Mom's bed.

"You need to eat more," he said as he retrieved the half eaten toast laying beside the dishes.

Ellen turned towards the doorway intending to peek in at Daisy. Mom smiled then said, "Daisy's sleeping, Ellen. Don't wake her."

"I won't."

She turned from the doorway and asked,

"What about Grandpa?"

"He's downstairs in his bedroom," said Dad as he started out the door with his tray. Dad looked back and said, "He's asking for you, Ellen."

Ellen hurried downstairs to the little room off of the kitchen that was Grandpa's. It was a warm room, heated by the wood stove in the kitchen. Grandpa's room was small but cozy with a wooden dresser for his clothes on one side and beside his single-sized bed was a night table with a photograph of Grandma and a well worn Bible on it. Some of his trousers and his jacket hung from hooks on the wall next to his bed.

Her grandpa looked older than when she left him. The skin on his face and hands was translucent with a slight blue and grey tinge. His white hair and pallid complexion made him disappear against the white pillow that he was laying on. His eyes were closed and she could hear his raspy and shallow breathing when she entered his bedroom.

"Grandpa," Ellen said quietly.

His eyelids fluttered, then opened when he heard Ellen's voice.

"Ellen, you're home. Thank goodness you're home." he croaked.

Ellen leaned up close to Grandpa.

"I'm here, Grandpa. Grandpa, you need to get well now."

Grandpa's face relaxed into a quiet small smile.

His faded blue eyes had a resigned faraway look.

"It's time for me to go home," he said.

"You are home, Grandpa."

Grandpa smiled a little wider and he patted Ellen's hand. It was a movement that was both wise and reassuring. He finally said, "Let me see you smile, Ellen. I want to see you smile."

The corners of her mouth turned up in a small smile but her blue eyes moistened as she said,

"I love you, Grandpa."

"Love you more," Grandpa answered.

"I think he needs some rest now, Ellen," her dad said quietly. Ellen stood up, then she turned to Grandpa and said, "Have a good rest, Grandpa. Don't let the bed bugs bite."

Grandpa's eyes were already closed and he was drifting off to sleep again, cradled by the music of his laboured breathing.

Later that evening, when Ellen was snuggled next to Daisy in their bed, she silently said a prayer of thanksgiving. Her whole family was together and they were all recovering from influenza. She slept well, her sister's quiet breathing a lullaby in the comfort and familiarity of her own surroundings.

Even before Ellen was fully awake, she could hear voices downstairs. The air outside of her bed was cool, so cool that she snuggled down underneath the quilts. Daisy was still sleeping beside her with Molly tucked under one of her arms. She listened again and this time she was sure she could hear Mom sobbing while talking to her dad.

"Grandpa!" she thought.

Ellen quickly climbed out of bed. She ignored the shock of cold that ran up through her feet when she stepped onto the floor and headed down the stairs and through to the kitchen where the voices were coming from.

"We'll need to get Dr. Albertson here again," said Dad.

Her dad was sitting in a kitchen chair with his bowed head in his hands.

"I can't believe this has happened," he said.

"What happened?" said Ellen as she entered the kitchen.

Her mom looked at her. She was dressed in her nightgown and her face was drawn with tears streaming down her cheeks.

"Why are you crying?" said Ellen.

"Oh, Ellen. It's your Grandpa."

"What about Grandpa?"

Ellen started for the door to Grandpa's bedroom.

"No, don't go in there. It's Grandpa. I'm sorry, Ellie, but your grandpa died last night in his sleep."

"He can't... No, he can't have. I just talked to him yesterday. He was okay. Couldn't the doctor save him?"

"No, Ellie. He had pneumonia, a complication of the flu. The doctor did all that he could for him."

"But he can't die," Ellen choked. A chill spread from her head to her toes and then back again. Even though she knew it was true she said, "I don't believe you!"

"He's with Grandma now. He's gone home," said Mom.

Ellen took giant steps towards the bedroom door and opened it. Grandpa looked like he was sleeping in his bed. He had a smile on his face but his chest wasn't rising and falling with the normal rhythm of breathing. In spite of the surging panic growing inside of her she could feel a calm and peaceful aura surrounding Grandpa. Ellen felt her dad's hands on her shoulders as they guided her out of the room and Ellen collapsed on his chest, tears streaming down her cheeks. The sobbing turned to a low wail.

Daisy, carrying Molly and William were watching open mouthed at the kitchen door. Mom gathered them up and ushered them into the parlour where she explained what had happened to Grandpa.

William tried to stifle the sobbing but finally gave way to it and Daisy, stunned, didn't really understand what had just happened. The three of them hugged. Mom holding tight to her children, wanted to comfort them.

Upstairs, as the day crawled on, Ellen's thoughts were blurred and confused behind her tired headache and swollen eyes. Like a stagnant pond without the rush of energizing water, she was inert, limp and heavy. She was only barely aware of the footsteps marching in and out of their house and the low murmuring voices downstairs. This time she didn't try to hear what was being said. She was numb and detached, tired from the residue illness that she was recovering from and the shock of losing her grandpa. It was a very long day, heavy with grief, one that she spent in her room unable to focus on anything or anyone. Every once in a while Daisy looked in the doorway. On her face was a frightened questioning look as she peered at Ellen. Then she quietly tiptoed into William's bedroom and they huddled together as though it would form a barrier to the sadness around them.

Later that night when it was time to go to sleep, Ellen turned to face Daisy in bed and finally began to speak into the inky darkness,

"Where's Molly?"

Daisy looked perplexed for a moment, then said,

"Oh, I forgot about her."

Daisy crawled out of bed and fumbled around in the dark until she found Molly. When she returned the bed felt stale and rumpled. Ellen's pillow was wrinkled and tear stained. Daisy tucked Molly safely under one arm and tried to find the comfort she was used to feeling beside Ellen in their bed. She continued,

"I'm worried, Ellen. Where did Grandpa go?"

Ellen shifted a little, hesitated, and then she began, "Daisy, I think he went to heaven."

"Is he ever coming back?"

"No, I don't think so."

"But how do you know?"

Daisy always looked up to her big sister. She thought Ellen was the smartest person she had ever met. Anytime she wanted to know anything she would ask Grandpa or Ellen. If anyone knew what happened to Grandpa it would be Ellen. Mom and Dad seemed to be so sad and she didn't know who else to ask. For as long as she could remember her grandpa had been there to help her and to answer her questions. He couldn't possibly go away just like that. She asked William but he just looked scared and wouldn't answer any of her questions.

"Daisy, do you remember when Loubelle, our milking cow, got sick. She died because she was too sick and Dad couldn't do anything for her. Dad and Grandpa buried her in the field. She went away and we never saw her again. Well, that's the same as Grandpa. He was just too sick to stay with us anymore."

"Are we going to bury Grandpa?"

"I'm not sure but I think so," said Ellen.

"If we die are they going to bury us too?"

"No one else is going to die, Daisy. Now let's go to sleep. We'll talk in the morning."

Daisy cuddled up to Ellen. She needed the reassurance of Ellen's warm body next to hers.

"Ellen, where's heaven? Is it far away?"

"I don't know, Daisy. I know it says in the Bible that when you go to heaven you live with God. I think that it is a long ways away."

"I wish he could stay with us forever."

"So do I, Daisy."

It took a long while for the two girls to drift off to sleep. Even the walls seemed to be stranger and colder. They whispered to Ellen that nothing would be the same again and a new kind of loneliness settled into her being. They would all miss their beloved Grandpa.

Chapter 8
Ellen's Guitar

In the weeks that followed, Ellen remained quiet and reflective.

"I'm going out to the barn," Ellen said to her mom after the midday dinner dishes were washed and dried.

"You're spending a lot of time out there. As long as you're going out, take this bucket of warm water for the chickens."

Ellen didn't answer. She grabbed the bucket and silently escaped out of the kitchen door and into the cold air. She didn't want to see the empty chair at the dinner table or Grandpa's bedroom that was slowly cleaned out, robbed of his personal items until there was only a bare room with a forlorn empty single bed sitting on the lonely wood floor. Ellen didn't know what happened to his things. She never asked. His funeral was a blur to Ellen. She remembered that there were a lot of people there and the single memory of the hymn *"Nearer My God to Thee"* resounded in her head.

As she opened the scratchy frozen wooden door to the chicken coop, she could hear soft happy clucking inside, a conversation of cooing, chirping and clicking. Their dozen laying hens inspected Ellen, held a debate, and then took turns dropping with a plop from their speckled perches. They fluffed their feathers and waddled over to her bucket to see what she had brought. After Ellen checked their feed bins she left the coop, placing the wooden bar across to securely lock the door.

The frozen footsteps made a path to the wooden cow barn, then past it to the horse stables. Ellen followed that path around the large log horse barn to the back where the hay was stacked against the outside wall. Leaning over she grabbed an armful of the cold hay and trudged inside with it. She made this trip many times as she found solace in looking after the animals, especially Nell.

Ellen felt the roughness of the aging wooden beam that bordered the stalls as she swung by just brushing the bridles and ropes that hung on a hook on the wall. The animal smells that were like a perfume to Ellen drifted through the air and into Ellen's thoughts while she dropped the hay into Nell's manger and checked her water to make sure it wasn't frozen. Nell greeted her friend with a gentle nuzzle into her neck and a soft whinny then bent down and lazily started chewing the golden hay that Ellen brought her. Ellen stroked her velvety neck and spoke quietly to her.

"They don't understand, Nell. I don't even know if they care."

There was a questioning look in Nell's eyes as she stopped chewing and studied Ellen.

"How about some treats? I'll get you some silage."

The silage was corn stalks and leaves that were chopped up and stored last fall, the fermented stew was both nourishing and satisfying. Nell nodded in approval. She enjoyed both the feast and the conversation Ellen brought to her.

Ellen slouched down into the bed of straw next to Nell's stall. She was staring off into space while twiddling with pieces of straw. Mom appeared from the shadows and silently sat down beside her and for a moment they were both still.

"I've never seen Nell so well groomed, Ellen. She's glowing like the Christmas star."

Ellen gave a half smile but wouldn't give her mom the satisfaction of a response.

"You know, we all miss him too," said Mom.

"No, you don't. You even cleaned out his room as though he was never there."

"It made us very sad to clean his room out but it was something that had to be done."

"Is there anything you would like?" said Mom.

There was another silence.

"He really didn't go away," Mom began again. "He loved you so much, Ellen. That love and all the memories are still alive. They're right here."

Mom placed two fingers together on Ellen's chest where her heart was. Ellen looked at her in surprise.

"All the love and memories of your grandpa are all there. He's living inside you. Nothing can take that away."

Ellen looked at her mom with tearing eyes and Mom continued,

"As long as you remember him, and as long as you honour him by loving your family and the people around you, your grandpa is still alive. He's a light that can shine through you, if you let it."

There was a peaceful moment of silence until Mom reached out and Ellen collapsed into the roundness of her expanding belly and soft warm breasts and a sob filled the air followed by more sobs. It was a relief to let go of her tightly held emotions and sink into her mom's knowing strength until Ellen was startled by a light thumping against her chest.

"What was that?"

Mom giggled and then put Ellen's hand around to her left side.

"It's the baby! You can feel the baby kicking."

"Can I feel it again?"

"Sure you can, Ellen."

"Is the baby coming soon?"

"This baby will be here in early spring."

"It sure is kicking and moving."

"That's why I think it's a boy."

Ellen put her head down to her mom's belly and tried to listen for the sound of the baby and the feel of its movement. She thought she might be able to hear its heartbeat.

Now more relaxed and excited about the baby, Ellen said to her mom,

"Could I have a picture of Grandpa. For my room, I mean. Then Daisy could look at it and William too sometimes."

"I don't know if we have one but some things got put away in a trunk. We'll have a look when we go back into the house. Let's go back, Ellen. I'd like to show you some of the new baby clothes I've made and we can look in the trunk together."

Ellen and her mom stood up and brushed some of the straw off of themselves, then arm in arm they walked out of the barn and followed the path back to the house.

Upstairs, in Mom and Dad's bedroom were beautifully sewn tiny white flannelette nightgowns with little ties at the back carefully folded and laying on her parent's bed. Beside them were white flannelette squares ready to be hemmed and a large piece of folded material beside them. Mom's black Singer sewing machine sat on the far wall of their bedroom. It was a treadle machine, one of Mom's prized possessions. There were some larger squares of patterned heavier flannelette on the extended arm of the sewing machine cabinet along with various spools of thread, scissors and a paper holder with straight needles in it.

Ellen fingered the small nightgowns marveling at their softness.

"Boy, are these ever small. Even Daisy's doll, Molly, is bigger than that," said Ellen.

"Do you remember when Daisy was that small?" asked Mom.

"No, I don't think she was ever that small."

"Well, she was. You know, Ellen, I could use some help hemming the baby's diapers and receiving blankets. It's a very simple stitch."

Ellen really enjoyed knitting the scarf. She was proud of the job she'd done when she gave it to her dad to wear. The peaceful clicking of the knitting needles, the texture of the wool and the feeling of accomplishment when it was finished gave her pleasure and satisfaction. She thought that she'd like to learn how to do the hand sewing.

"Yes, if you could show me. I think I can do it."

"All right. I'll show you but first let's have a look inside of that trunk of your grandpa's.

The trunk was hidden in a far corner of their bedroom with a white crocheted cover on top of it. Mom removed the cover, unlocked and opened the lid of the trunk. It was an old patchy blue trunk, with brass coloured corners on it and a matching heavy locking mechanism that swung up and down. They peered inside of it inhaling the odour of stale air and mothballs. The top was filled with a blue patterned tray that fit into it. They carefully lifted it out and put it on the bed. Grandpa's Bible was there as well as the photograph of Grandma. There were some shiny medals along with some official looking papers in a small box that Ellen picked up. She opened it and admiring the contents she said,

"Where did these come from?"

"The Boer War, I believe," answered Mom.

"I never knew Grandpa was in a war," said Ellen.

"He wasn't. These were your Uncle Albert's, your dad's older brother."

"Is this Grandpa in this picture?" Ellen said picking up an ancient photograph.

"No, it's your Uncle Albert."

"I don't know him."

"That's because he died in the war. I don't think your grandpa ever stopped missing him. He was the oldest you know."

After a moment she continued,

"He looked very much like your grandpa."

Ellen held up a yellowed photograph of a young man in a uniform carrying a gun. He had a hat with one side bent upwards and was standing with a group of other young men. She studied it for a while. In school she had learned a little bit about the Boer War but she never realized that anyone from her family had participated in it.

"Here's another picture. I think this is Grandpa and Grandma."

"That looks like it's their wedding picture."

The photograph was beautifully mounted on a heavy dark paper board. Its creamy white background enhanced the formal sitting of a youthful petite dark haired woman and a slender tall, suited and bright eyed man. Her grandpa was clean shaven exposing a handsome young face that was open and smiling.

"They look so young!" Ellen declared.

"Yes, they were young. They were married for a long time."

"That one can go on the mantle in the parlour," said Mom. She held it with both hands and gazed lovingly at it.

Ellen slowly went through the rest of the contents of the trunk's tray. There was his gold pocket watch, his wedding ring and a brown felt hat her grandpa always wore. Ellen fingered the warm smoothness of the brim and her stomach lurched with the memory of her grandpa's hat that hung on a hook when he wasn't wearing it. There was a packet of letters written on delicate paper and bound with a narrow blue ribbon. Ellen picked up a funny looking piece of pink paper, yellowed on the corners, with a childish drawing of a horse on one side. It said on the back, "Happy Birthday, Grandpa, love Ellen."

"He kept this," Ellen said.

"I remember when I made it a long time ago."

"There's something else," Mom said.

"This was under his bed. I don't have any idea where it came from. Your grandpa said he was going to fix it up one day and play it, but of course he never did. It's been under there for a while I think."

Mom held up a guitar and Ellen, fascinated, looked it over from one side to the other. The wood was still glowing but there were patches where the finish was worn off. There were no strings on it and the keys at the back were chipped. One key was broken off altogether. The body of the guitar was cracked causing its belly to be misshaped. Its limitations didn't dampen Ellen's interest as she turned it over and over, looking intently at the instrument.

"Can I have it?" she asked Mom.

"I don't see why not," Mom answered.

"Wait," said Mom. "This is a Hawaiian steel guitar. There has to be a steel somewhere that you slide up and down the neck of the guitar when you're playing it. Let's look and see if we can find it."

"There's a funny piece of metal in the trunk," said Ellen.

"That's it," said Mom.

"Now we need a pick. They're plastic things that you play the strings with."

"I don't see any."

"We might be able to find some later."

"Thanks, Mom," Ellen said as she darted out of the room carrying the guitar.

Now the focal point of Ellen's determination, the guitar was slowly transformed. She and her dad brought the guitar to a neighbour, Mr. Wallace. Mr. Wallace was experienced with repairing violins.

He picked up the guitar and put it on his wooden work bench. Then he studied it turning it over a few times and said,

"This crack in the body is pretty wide but I think the glue will hold it. Here, Ellen. Hold this while I try to fill it."

Ellen's gaze was fixed while Mr. Wallace squeezed the white glue into the crack along the outside of the body of the guitar. Ellen wondered if it was even possible to bring the instrument back to its original shape.

"Okay now. Hold it steady. I'm going to clamp it together."

As the clamps were tightened the guitar's belly slowly squeezed together and excess white glue bubbled at the crack and spilled over onto its shiny surface. Ellen watched as Mr. Wallace picked up a cloth rag and wiped the extra glue from the guitar.

"Now we have to wait. The glue needs time to dry. Just leave it here and if you can come next Saturday we'll finish with it."

The glue dried clear and invisible. Once the clamps were removed the guitar rejoiced in its original shape. Even though it looked perfect to Ellen it still needed strings and keys.

"The next time I'm in town I can order what you need to finish the guitar," said Mr. Wallace.

Ellen's eyes widened and she said,

"I don't have any money to pay for it though."

"Maybe we could work something out. I have a lot of chores that need to be done. I could sure use some help around here. Do you think you might be interested in working for them?"

"Sure, I can do almost anything," Ellen declared.

A few weeks later the parts for her guitar arrived on the train from Winnipeg. Ellen worked for Mr. Wallace on Saturdays. He kept her busy cleaning the barns and tidying up his workshop for him. Mr. Wallace smiled to himself. He felt that he was lucky to have found such an energetic and pleasant worker.

When it was time to take her guitar home he said,

"You're going to have a problem with carrying this guitar around."

"I think I can manage," said Ellen.

"This might make it a lot easier," said Mr. Wallace and he looked underneath his wooden bench and pulled out a black guitar case. It was an old one, worn on the seams and the corners but it was sturdy and the metal locks worked fine. Best of all there was a strong handle on it.

"Here, let's see if it fits in here."

Ellen couldn't believe her good fortune. Her guitar fit inside as though they were made to go together. The inside of the case was like new. Its blue and white patterned lining welcomed her renovated instrument.

"Look, it's even got a little compartment for the steel," said Ellen. "I'll work to pay for it."

"No need, Ellen. An old fellow, can't remember his name, brought it in with his violin that he wanted fixed. He said that he didn't want it and someone might be able to use it. It's just been sitting here gathering dust ever since."

"Thanks, Mr. Wallace. I'll take good care of it."

Ellen picked up her guitar case now heavy with its contents and balancing it with the neck up, gratefully walked out of his shop.

Proud of her accomplishment, Ellen brought her guitar home to show her family. Her mom's blue eyes lit up with delight when she saw what they had done with the guitar. She ran her hand over the smooth wood on the surface admiring both her daughter and the wooden instrument. There was a secret wish hatching in her mind. The whole family gathered in the parlour, curious to see Ellen's new guitar.

Dad brought out his violin, tucked it under his chin and played an impromptu spirited rendition of *"Red River Valley."* Dad kept perfect time tapping with the heel of his foot while Mom swayed back and forth in celebration of the happy rhythms.

William and Daisy watched Ellen in astonishment. They had heard their dad play the violin before and they heard Mom play the piano at the Christmas concert. Now they wondered what kind of sound would be forthcoming from this guitar that Ellen brought home.

Daisy giggled, relief washing over her. It seemed like it had been a long time since Mom and Dad were this happy.

The musical notes bounced through the parlour like bright and sparkly sunbeams playfully lighting their spirits with delight and gaiety. Only William sat quietly in a corner looking detached from the merry making. His gaze followed his dad to Ellen, then back to Dad, and with a half hidden sneer, he thought, "What's so great about a stupid guitar, anyway?"

Ellen and her dad sat through a blissful Sunday afternoon working together to tune her guitar. With her dad's help she turned the keys until the right sounds emerged. The metal rings of the picks slipped loosely around her slender fingers. He then showed her how to hold the round shiny steel with her left hand and slide it up and down the neck of the guitar to make the coordinating notes.

Ellen fell in love with the rolling twangy sounds her new guitar made. Once she understood how it was done she kept playing some notes over and over again, her mind totally focused and smiling inwardly. Her guitar would become a very special friend, one that she would cherish for a long time.

Woven into Ellen's mosaic of home and school were hours of practice on her guitar whenever she could steal some free moments. They were special moments. Sometimes when Ellen was hungry for an approving audience she took her guitar out to the horse barn, set herself down in the hay with the guitar on her lap and played for Nell. Mom showed her some chords to play and Ellen, enjoying the challenge, worked very hard to perfect them.

I wonder what that is, she thought on one of her trips to the barn.

There was a pencil thin column of smoke rising from the far side of the wood shed that was opposite the horse stables. She stopped and took a better look. William's face appeared from behind the shed. Their gaze locked, then William quickly disappeared back behind the shed. Ellen wondered what he was doing there but she was anxious to play the song that she learned and continued on to see Nell in the stables.

"I learned a song, Nell. It goes like this."

Ellen sang *"That's an Irish Lullaby"* while she played the chords to the song. Her chording was hesitant at first when she had to change notes but Ellen quickly became more fluent as the song came to a conclusion. Nell came to the entrance of the stall, ears twitching, and looked at Ellen with interest. Nell's head bobbed and she whinnied softly in time to the music.

"What do you think, Nell? Sounds pretty good, huh?"

Nell responded to Ellen's enthusiasm and she circled around the stall and back to the opening in agreement.

Winter trudged along, the nights slowly giving way to longer days. The bold and outspoken air grudgingly and hesitantly began to thaw as the earth travelled towards warmer and kinder spring days.

Chapter 9
Crime and Punishment

"What are you doing?"

William jumped and turned to see Daisy looking at him from the corner of the wood shed.

"Where did you come from?" William responded. He tried to hide his homemade cigarette behind his back, but the oversized stogie made from dried leaves rolled in newspaper was leaving a tell-tale trail of smoke from behind William.

"I'm going to tell Mom what you're doing."

"I'm not doing anything."

"Yes, you are. You're smoking. Mom'll be mad at you."

"No. I'm not."

At that point the glowing cylinder burned right down and stung his fingers. William, startled, yelped and shook his hand dropping the dying butt onto the cold frosted ground.

"I want to try too."

William stomped on the last of the glowing embers of the cigarette.

"No, you're just a little kid. You can't smoke."

"Yes, I can and I'm not a little kid. Let me try too."

"Go back to the house, Daisy."

"If you don't let me try I'm going to tell Mom what you're doing."

"Go back to the house, damn it!"

"Huhh... I'm going to tell Mom that you're smoking AND swearing."

"Oh, all right. Just don't move while I make another one."

Daisy observed from her assigned distance until curiosity got the best of her and she huddled in closer to watch William while he tore off a rectangular piece of paper from the old newspaper he'd hidden between the cut firewood. Then from the back pocket of his overalls he pulled his homemade tobacco made with dried poplar leaves he and his friend from school, George, gathered from mulch under the trees.

William and George were delighted when the frozen and brittle mulch they found crumbled easily in their hands forming what they considered to look like tobacco.

William filled the center of the paper with the leaves, then carefully rolled it up while Daisy looked on.

"Where did you get that?"

"I made it. What do you think?"

Daisy watched in fascination. She could barely contain her excitement at being included as a co-conspirator.

"That doesn't look very good. Are you sure it's going to work?"

"Quiet, Daisy. I know how to do it."

"How do you know?"

"George showed me. He says he does it all the time."

Daisy continued to watch him with interest.

William was clumsy trying to roll up the cigarette between his two hands. One end was left open with the leaves showing while he tucked in the end that he was going to put in his mouth to puff on the cigarette.

When he put together what he thought was a satisfactory cigarette he leaned against the firewood and felt the sunlit soaked chunk that was weeping half frozen tears of thawing moisture when it poked him in the back. With his head bent downward William adopted a pose that he assumed suggested both boldness and sophistication.

It wasn't a large woodshed. It was open at one end where the family's supply of firewood that kept them warm through the bitter cold winter was stored. The wood was chopped and split into foot long quarters, then stacked and left to dry. At the back of the shed where William and Daisy were collaborating, some snow crusted firewood was left stacked outside in the open air against the back wall. On the ground was a large heavy wood splitting block with remnants of spear like kindling laying where wood was split before being stored. Dad's axe and his mallet were leaning against the block and his weighty metal splitter lay on the ground beside the wood block.

Every few moments William glanced around at the horse barn, which was about eight meters away from the shed. He'd seen Ellen go in there and he didn't want her to find out what he was doing.

"Here's how you do it."

William pulled out a red covered book of matches from his other pocket.

"Where did you get those?"

"From the kitchen. What do you think?"

Daisy, mesmerized by the whole process, watched as William put one end of the very large cigarette into his mouth and with the other hand flipped open the matchbook cover. Then she heard the crack when William struck the match, igniting the small flame and releasing the odour of sulphur into the cold air. Black smoke curled upwards from the red glow at the end of his homemade tube announcing that the dried leaves and newspaper were slowly burning. William pretended to inhale then knowingly puffed in shallow breaths.

"My turn," squealed Daisy.

"Not yet. You don't know how."

"You promised! You said I could try."

"All right, but be careful. Smoking is for grown-ups you know."

William took the fat burning cigarette from his mouth with his first two fingers and held it up to Daisy. She grabbed it from him with one hand.

"Not like that. Like this."

William demonstrated how he held the cigarette between two fingers. Daisy, anxious to try, grabbed the stogie and quickly shoved one end into her mouth. Before William could say anything more she sucked in a big breath and inhaled the large column of black smoke.

Her eyes grew as large as saucers. Stunned, she winced and with puffed cheeks she held her breath while tears welled up in her astonished eyes.

"Let it out!" he screamed. "Daisy, breathe, let it out."

William panicked. He slapped her on the back and Daisy started to cough letting out the vile black smoke she'd inhaled. She continued coughing while her rosy complexion first turned pale then a sickening green. Her eyes stung and she couldn't stop coughing and struggling for air. When she was finally able to speak, she gasped,

"I'm telling Mom."

She let out a low wail.

"It hurts," she choked. "I'm telling."

"No, don't tell Mom."

William tried to rub her back and begged her to stop crying.

"I'm telling," she sobbed and turned and ran towards the house.

William dropped the burning cigarette on the ground near the chopping block and kindling, then bolted after her but Daisy was on a mission. She was too quick for him to stop her.

Mom was standing in the open doorway when Daisy ran right into her. Tears were streaming down her face and she was still coughing and sputtering when she buried herself into Mom's waist. Mom lifted Daisy's chin with her hand and peered at Daisy's face. Mom inhaled deeply and sniffed around her head. She smelled smoke on Daisy.

William, running, came to a quick halt, knowing full well that he was in trouble. He looked for somewhere to hide but he was too close. Mom saw him and when their eyes connected she frowned at him suspiciously, then her face contorted with anger as she noted his guilty face. She said,

"William, what did you do to your sister? Daisy, tell me what happened. Were you smoking?"

Daisy was still choking and coughing but managed to point her finger at William and say,

"He did it. He's smoking."

"William!!!" Mom's voice rose to a higher pitch.

"She wanted to. Honest. It was her idea." William pleaded.

William knew that look on his mom's face and realized that it was no use. He turned and ran towards the front of the house. The ground was slippery and he was just barely able to recover his balance when he skidded past the side windows. Mom was in hot pursuit.

"William," she screeched. "You come back here, you little devil. What did you do to your sister?"

Mom wasn't able to successfully run after and catch him but she was so furious she tried anyway. While William was scrambling around to the front of the house, Mom decided that she would meet him on the other side when he came around. She continued to yell at him.

"William, you get back here! Oh boy, are you in trouble now!"

As Mom approached the other side of the house, William rounded the front side at the same time, saw Mom and like a fast train approaching the station, he skidded to a halt. His arms were flailing in the air to stop himself from slipping and falling on his back. He recovered and ran back to the front again. Mom also turned and rounded the back of the house. Absorbed in her anger, she bumped into and nearly tripped over a broom handle that was leaning against the kitchen door. She grabbed the handle that was missing its broom, and now fully armed and very angry, she continued her chase, wildly waving the broom handle in the air.

"William, don't you dare run away from me!"

Mom's voice became louder and shriller and her face turned red with exertion.

Daisy stopped sobbing and watched wide eyed as her mom chased William back and forth from side to side of the house. She'd never seen her mom so angry. William was like a scared rabbit darting back and forth to avoid being caught. Now it was just a question of who would tire out first. On his next trip towards the side of the house he was surprised to run right into Dad who was working in the cattle barn and heard the commotion going on between William and Mom. Dad grabbed him by the hair and yelled,

"So, you like to smoke, do you? You like to give cigarettes to your little sister, do you?"

Dad's words were emphasized with quick jerks on William's scalp. William didn't dare wriggle too much. He just grimaced and cowered from his dad's interrogation.

Their exchange was halted abruptly with shrill cries from Ellen.

"Dad, come quick! Dad! FIRE!"

Hot hungry red flames licked the back of the firewood shed then reached up to the sky probing for more nourishment. With unbelievable speed the flames grew. The residue of billowing black smoke rose in columns into the soft cobalt sky overhead. The chords of pale firewood edged with heavy coarse bark stored in the shed were very dry and they drew the flames to them. Sparks crackled, popped and glowed like fireflies as the ravenous flames consumed their meal then flew over the glowing wood shed searching for more.

Dad dropped his grip on William and groaned when he saw the smoke rising at the back shed. The woodshed was close to the horse barn. Dad yelled to Ellen.

"Get the horses out of the barn!"

"Ellen," he yelled louder as he ran. "The horses. Get the horses out of the barn."

Ellen heard him and hurried inside the barn. She heard Nell's warning snorts as she paced in circles in her stall. Nell`s eyes were wide and alert in her upright jerking head. Her forward ears listened to the crackling fire outside and her flaring nostrils grew sensitive to the irritating invasion of threatening black smoke.

Ellen slipped the halter on Nell, then another one on Sal, opened the stall doors and led them both outside and away from the barn. Then she ran back to the barn to rescue their two dark Belgian horses that were also in the barn and to carry out her precious guitar in its case.

The cracking and popping that the dry firewood made when sparks flew into the air and the heavy smell of smoke permeated through the atmosphere that was like a furnace transforming the woodshed into a black skeleton of ash and red embers. Increasing heat travelled through the air in waves distorting the blue sky above.

Behind the shed where the fire started were the charred remnants of firewood and kindling crackling and smoldering on the frozen ground. What remained of the wood block was glowing while flames attacked and licked its perimeter. Dad's axe handle was consumed in flames that avoided the red iridescent metal head and heavy splitter.

For a few seconds, Mom and Daisy were frozen in horror. After telling Daisy to stay at the house, Mom headed to the cow barn as fast as she could to get the gunny sacks that were stored at the back of the cow barn. Dad was already at the well where he started to pump up water into a bucket to douse the fire with. William was right behind him. Dad barked at William,

"If you're old enough to smoke, you're old enough to fight fire! Now grab this handle and start pumping."

It was too late to save the woodshed. Now he had to make sure that the horse barn didn't dissolve in flames as well. Dad grabbed the full bucket and poured it on the landed sparks on the side of the horse barn. The adrenalin rush gave Dad energy that he didn't know he possessed. He ran back and forth from the well as though being chased by a wild cat while yelling at William to pump faster.

"Don't stop. Keep going, boy. We have to get that fire out."

William's arms felt like they would fall off any minute but he didn't dare stop or complain. He kept up to his dad's pace without flinching.

Breathless, Mom arrived close to the woodshed with her armload of gunny sacks. After rescuing the horses, Ellen joined her mom and grabbed a sack to beat any landed sparks of fire into submission. The four of them worked furiously, their hair was damp with sweat and their breathing was rapid and painful with the inhaled smoke but they hurried on throughout the afternoon until all of the flying sparks had died out. The roar in the woodshed died down, simmering and smelling of ash and soot. Its fragile blackened brittle frame collapsed inwardly consumed by the red hot incinerator in the center of the crumpled woodshed. When they finally relaxed, resigned to losing the woodshed, they were spent and worn.

"You're exhausted, Kate," said Dad.

"There's nothing more that we can do," said Mom.

Mom leaned against the horse barn. An ash stained, ragged gunny sack drooped from one of her hands and desperately dragged on the ground. There were tears of fatigue showing in her eyes and new lines of weariness were evident on her drawn face. Dad put his arm around her and hugged her close.

"Go into the house and lay down, please, Kate."

Mom closed her eyes and took a deep breath. She could feel her heart beating rapidly and she wrapped one hand around her middle and waited for the familiar thumping of her unborn child. At last, it came. Mom heaved a sigh and slowly walked back towards the house. As she passed William, she put one hand on his shoulder, then without saying a word she continued to walk through the back door and into the kitchen.

William sat down on the cold and damp ground beside the pump handle. His downcast eyes were red rimmed from the sting of the smoke and the tears that he tried to wipe from his dirt and tear stained face. He didn't feel bold or sophisticated anymore.

"How am I ever going to fix this?" he thought. "Maybe I should run away or something."

Dad quietly sat down beside him.

"Dad, I'm really sorry. I didn't mean for this to happen."

Neither of them stirred for a moment. When he finally spoke, Dad put his arm around William's shaking shoulders and said,

"I know you didn't."

William broke down into sobs. He cried as though his overfull heart was spilling out the bottled up damn of emotions. The flood of tears drained his grief and fears.

"Why did he have to die anyway?"

Dad took a deep breath, then said,

"I don't know, William, but we all miss him too. It's going to be all right, you know."

William felt the texture of his dad's jacket and the strength of his chest against his flushed cheek. His regret made him feel small and humble in his dad's arms.

"What are we going to do?" he asked his dad.

"Well, we need the wood to keep us warm. I guess we'll have to replace it. I'm afraid that you're going to have to work hard to cut and split firewood. We need it to stay warm."

"I can do it, Dad."

Dad gave his shoulders a squeeze and said,

"I guess that's punishment enough."

They got up together and went inside the house. Dad still had one arm around his shoulder. It was an unspoken gesture of forgiveness.

Over the next few weeks William spent every spare minute working with his dad cutting wood and splitting it. Then it was piled in layers in a row behind the barn. The work was hard on his youthful body but as time went on he felt stronger and more confident. When he raised the mallet and swung it as hard as he could the round piece of wood cracked then split, wide and triumphant, in two. Then smaller pieces were split off of it with the repaired axe. William loved the happy chatter with his dad at mealtimes when they finished working at the woodpile. Gone was the guilt and fear of a young boy. He was now wearing the smile in his eyes and the calm confidence of a young man.

Chapter 10
Rotten Ice

Whatever will become of me thought Ellen. She was sitting on a stump in the cool crisp spring air outdoors. That question was on her mind a lot lately. Her blue eyes had a faraway look as she attempted to look into the future.

I'd really like to start Grade 9 in September but I don't know if I'll be able to. She was almost finished Grade 8 but their little one room school didn't go any further than that.

I don't think my parents can afford to send me to the high school in Portage la Prairie. Ellen took a deep breath and let it out. I know a place where I could live and go to school she thought hopefully. Miss Larson said there was a boarding house not far from the school and that she could give my parents the address for it. How will I ever see all of those places in the book if I can't graduate and earn my way?

This thought was interrupted by a broad tailed hummingbird that balanced and hovered just in front of her eyes. It paused just a moment then darted forward then backwards again. She heard its tiny wings making a whirring sound as they beat the air. Through the blur of its pulsating wings Ellen caught a glimpse of its iridescent red throat, green head and its long slender straight bill.

"I bet you know what you're doing next fall," Ellen spoke aloud to the hummingbird.

The hummingbird circled in sharp quick movements then hovered once more in front of Ellen. Its wings seemed to disappear in its flight. It seemed to say to Ellen, Don't worry, everything will be all right.

Ellen's worrisome thoughts continued as she remembered hearing a conversation between her mom and dad last night. The property taxes still needed to be paid by this summer and they hadn't been able to save enough money for them.

I wonder what will happen if we don't have the money to pay them thought Ellen.

Ellen didn't like to think about Mr. Beettle's interest in Nell either.

They wouldn't dare sell Nell to pay the taxes. At least I hope not. Last Saturday when Ellen rode Nell to Pratt General Store to get the mail, Mr. Beettle was there, smiling with his new gleaming white teeth at her. She scowled back at him when he walked over to Nell and looking down she refused to answer his greeting. He had a gleam in his eye that Ellen didn't like. She thought, stay away from my Nell. She's not for sale.

Ellen came alive to the rough texture of the stump that she was sitting on and in the morning light she felt the crisp spirited wind on her face and loved the way it played with her hair, picking up strands and swirling it around her head. It felt good, fresh and clean. Above her were magnificent thick clouds in various shades of soft blues and greys. They were like a woolen blanket that kept the earth warm while it slept through the night. Then they spread out and moved, puffing and swaying in the wind that swept across the wide expanse of the prairie sky.

A streaked brown and spotted meadowlark sitting on a fencepost nearby was singing welcome back to the grasslands that were slowly being reclaimed from the frozen winter crust.

New energy and unrest stirred in her chest as she surveyed the gently rolling prairie hills around her. They seemed to go on forever, pulling her to follow the gravel road that trailed through the receding puddles of frozen ice and snow and patches of pale golden grasses.

Ellen was jolted back from her reverie when she heard a loud crack booming through the air followed by several small crashing sounds.

It must be the rotten ice she thought. Grandpa used to say that when the ice was warming up it would crack and shift and bang into other chunks of ice close to shore. Grandpa said that the loudest cracks came when the ice hit the river bank.

Another loud crack sang out into the air.

I remember that he said that old ice was weakened and not very safe. He called it 'rotten ice.'

Ellen's thoughts were pulled away by the sound of a horse galloping in the distance. Moving towards her like a scurrying ant was a wagon pulled by a white and brown palomino horse. She studied them intently as it disappeared down a rolling hill then emerged at the top of it.

I wonder who that is.

Ellen got up from the stump and with one hand shaded her eyes from the sky and the cool breeze, then slowly walked towards the approaching wagon.

I don't think I've seen them before she thought.

"Whoa," cried the driver, and the wagon came to a stop almost beside Ellen. Seated in the wagon was a sturdy looking lady. She was wearing a heavy grey coat that was buttoned improperly lifting one side of her coat higher than the other. The gaps it produced revealed a pink printed dress underneath. A green woolen hat sat on top of her large fleshy round face. Her greying hair was tied back in a bun at the nape of her neck. Her voice was loud and gravelly, abrasive to Ellen's ears.

"Come and grab my bag," she said to Ellen.

"Who are you?" Ellen responded.

"Never mind that. I'm here to see your mom."

"Why do you need to see my mom?" Ellen questioned.

"Stop asking questions, girl. Take my bag into the house and then come and tend to my horse."

Ellen could hear her heavy breaths as the woman climbed out of the wagon. She had a crooked gait, walking heavily from one leg to the other with her shoulders moving up and down in time to her steps as she moved up the path towards the front door of their house. Ellen stared after her. She was sure she'd never seen her before. The woman turned back to Ellen and said,

"The bag. Get the bag, girl."

Ellen recovered in spite of her curiosity and grabbed her printed canvas bag from the wagon and followed her up the path and through their front door. As soon as they entered their hallway the woman asked,

"Where's your Mother?"

William was coming down the stairs as she was speaking and he said,

"She's up here. She's in her bedroom."

The woman grabbed hold of the railing with one hand and lifted one heavy foot onto the first stair.

"Show me the way then, boy."

Ellen looked up at William and asked from behind the woman,

"Where's Dad?"

The woman turned back and looked at Ellen. Between puffs of air and a tilt of her chin she addressed Ellen.

"Your dad came to get me for your mom. He should be here any minute. I was halfway through my washing and had to leave it but I came right away. I hardly took the time to put my hat and coat on."

An awareness passed over Ellen's face and she thought, the baby. Is the baby coming?

At that moment they heard the kitchen door open. Following the sounds of footsteps, Dad's silhouette appeared in the hallway.

"I'm so glad you're here, Mrs. Vanders," he said to the woman. "It didn't take you long to get here."

"Yes, well, let's stop jabbering. I need to examine your wife."

"This way," said Dad and he stepped ahead of her and led the way up the squeaking stairs to their bedroom. From the top of the stairs Dad said,

"I think you two should wait downstairs."

Ellen left William and Daisy in the parlour and hurried outdoors to look after Mrs. Vander's horse.

Molly was propped up against their sofa while Daisy was busy setting up her toy tea set.

"Do you want to play dolls?"

"No, I don't. That's for baby girls."

Daisy rolled her eyes. She pretended to pour tea into a tiny china teacup then offered it to Molly with some pretend cookies. William didn't take his eyes off of the doorway. Absent minded, he kept rolling his marbles from one hand to another while he waited for someone to tell him what was happening to Mom.

Ellen walked back to the house, deep in thought.

What did that lady want with her mom? I think it has something to do with the new baby that was coming. I'm sure that's it. I hope everything is okay. Is this lady a doctor?

When Ellen joined William and Daisy in the parlour, her uneasiness weighed like a heavy stone anchoring her to the sofa she was sitting on. She examined and counted the patterns the blue cone flowers that were meandering up and down on the wallpaper made and continually shifted her nervous legs while she played with some loose threads on a cushion sitting on their sofa. Finally, Dad came downstairs to speak to the three children. Even though their eyes asked a dozen questions they were silent while they waited for their dad to explain.

"Mrs. Vanders is a person who delivers babies," Dad began. "I think your mom is going to have the baby soon so I went and got her to come and help."

"Is she a midwife, Dad?" Ellen asked.

Dad smiled. He was unaware that his daughter was knowledgeable about these things.

"Yes, I suppose she is."

"Where's Dr. Albertson?" asked Ellen.

"He got called to an accident at the McCaulie farm across the river. I'm not sure what happened and I don't know if I can get word to him with the ice starting to break up in the river."

They could hear the sound of footsteps moving back and forth upstairs. Then they heard the door opening and closing.

"Mr. Graham!" the coarse voice called from the top of the stairs. "I need to talk to you."

Dad, taking two steps at a time, hurried back upstairs to see what Mrs. Vanders wanted.

Ellen could hear the low murmur of conversation in the distance. She strained to hear what they were saying but she was only able to distinguish a few words between the murmuring. She heard Mrs. Vanders say in her loud voice,

"I can't," and "breach."

A frown creased in Ellen's brow as she quietly tried to discern what exactly was being said and what it meant.

Breach, she thought. She concentrated hard for a few moments and started to remember a year ago when their calves were born. One little calf had a difficult time with the birthing because its feet were coming first and Dad had to help their cow give birth to the calf because she was having such a strenuous time. She heard her dad say that the calf was born breach.

Oh my, she thought. Is that what's happening to Mom?

Ellen sucked in a breath and held it for a few moments while she tried to remember what the stern long words in Mom's blue medical book said but she couldn't recollect what she had read. She paced back and forth from the parlour to the stairway, waiting for Dad to emerge from the darkness upstairs. The minutes felt like hours before the whining stairs announced his return to the parlour.

"What is it, Dad?" said Ellen.

Dad's eyes, weighed under with heavy thoughts were downcast. Finally, he said,

"Ellen, you need to look after things while I'm gone."

"Gone! You can't leave! Where are you going,

Dad?" Ellen nearly shouted as she followed her Dad into the kitchen.

"Dad, tell me. Where are you going? What's wrong with Mom?" Ellen's bottom lip started to quiver and a salty tear puddled in her eye as the panic set in. Dad turned to face her.

"Ellen, try not to worry. Mom will be fine. I need to go and get Dr. Albertson." Then as if to himself he quietly said,

"Everything will be all right. It has to be."

"But, how can you? He's on the other side of the river, isn't he?"

Dad looked directly at Ellen, their eyes connecting, to reinforce what he was saying.

"I'll get him. Now don't you fret. Just watch your sister and give Mrs. Vanders any help she needs. I'm going to take Nell and we'll both be back as soon as we can. I talked to Mrs. Vanders and she'll stay until I return with the doctor."

Ellen was trembling and she brokenly said,

"Please, Dad. Be careful."

Then as a tear released from her blue eyes she said,

"Dad, I'm scared."

Cold, icy tentacles of fear held her in their grip until Dad took Ellen by the shoulders and hugged her to him. She sunk into his chest and her tears dampened the rough texture of his brown wool jacket.

"Now, Ellie. Try not to worry. I'll be back as soon as I can. Maybe you can start dinner."

When Dad let go, he grabbed his brown suede hat that hung on a hook. His face was drawn and he had a distant look. As Ellen raised her hand in goodbye her mind was swimming with uncertainties. How was her dad going to get across the rotten ice in the river? What will happen to her mom and the new little baby? Ellen barely heard his footsteps and the slam of the kitchen door when Dad sharply closed it behind himself.

Outside in the cool spring air that was as fresh and clean as a rushing creek, Dad's pace quickened as he approached the horse barn. In the distance he heard the familiar booming and cracking of the ice as it shifted from its cold frozen prison. With new energy and focus he started mentally rehearsing the journey he was about to take. He quickly put the saddle on Nell all the while talking to her.

"We've got a job to do, Nell. You and I. I need you to be fast and brave."

Dad quickly mounted her and without wasting a second flicked the reins and gave her a poke in the ribs.

"Giddap," he called out as he urged her on.

Snow and yellowed grass flew up from her hooves as they galloped down the gravel road then through the fields towards the Assiniboine River. In communion, man and horse sailed through the rolling fields as though they were air borne. They covered the two miles to the narrowest part of the river with all of the speed and agility that Nell could muster.

"Whoa," Dad said pulling up on the reins.

The river bank was a confused frozen tangle of blue and white crusted logs and debris. Nell had to carefully pick her way through to get to the water's edge. Nell's ears perked up at the sound of the rushing water beneath the frozen icy crust that covered the river. Then she sniffed the ground around her and the air that was infused with the sweet smell of damp earth. The clouds had rolled away leaving behind the clear wide cobalt sky that framed the pale misty blue and grey ice that lay ahead.

"What do you think?" Dad said aloud to Nell.

Nell sniffed again, then raised her head in affirmation.

"Okay, girl. I guess this is it then."

Dad dismounted and the two of them gingerly stepped onto the ice and carefully moved around the cracks. They both examined the ice for grey and splotchy areas where the ice had thawed, then froze again making the ice weak. They zigzagged across with Dad leaning down close to the ice to see where they were stepping. They were almost across the river when Dad felt the ice shifting underneath them. Dad, leading with the reins, hurried Nell to the other side where the ice looked a little more stable.

"Come on, Nell. Let's go."

They moved quickly to safety on the other side. Dad mounted Nell again and she struggled through the debris and snowy mounds. They were no sooner safely on the other side when they both were startled by a very large cracking sound. Dad pulled on her reins. He could feel the damp sweat beneath his hat as he turned to look back at the river. A large wide crack threateningly grew and spread from the other side. A piece of ice shattered away from the crack and rose into the air revealing a glassy dark pool underneath it.

"Let's go, Nell. We've no time to waste."

Nell climbed up to the gravel road and was soon galloping towards the McCaulie farm. The fields were a blur of pale yellow and dirty white snow patches and the occasional naked fuzzy tree. As they raced forward it seemed that the wind at their backs gave them extra energy and thrust to quickly cover the seven miles to the McCaulie farmhouse.

Chapter 11
Tommy

"Daisy, come and help me do the breakfast dishes," said Ellen.

Daisy put her tiny teacup down and looked at Ellen standing in the parlour doorway.

"Why do I need to help?"

"Because the kitchen is a mess and it needs to be cleaned up before I make our dinner. You can bring your play teacups in and we'll wash them too. Dad said that I'm to look after things. Please, Daisy come and help."

"Why can't William help?"

"Because he's feeding the chickens."

"Okay, I'm coming."

Ellen busied herself by pouring hot water from the wood stove and soap into the dishpan. She scraped the leftover porridge into the garbage pail, then sunk the ceramic bowls into the hot soapy water. Following the bowls came the large spoons and glasses.

"I want to wash," said Daisy.

"Sure, just roll up your sleeves so you don't get all wet."

Daisy did as she was asked. Then she slowly swirled the soap around in a circle flicking the bubbles with her little fingers. Ellen picked up a mug half full of cold coffee, the cream floating and crusted on the inside perimeter of the cup and dumped it into the dish pan with the rest of the dirty dishes.

"Ellen, I'm worried. Is Mom going to be all right?"

"I'm sure that Mom'll be just fine."

"But I thought Grandpa would be all right and he died."

"Daisy, don't worry. Mom isn't going to die."

"Are you sure, Ellen?"

Ellen wondered if she was sure of anything. Daisy's concerns echoed her own worries. With shaky legs and trembling hands, an unease she felt as though bracing for a terrible storm, she did her best to reassure and distract Daisy and keep her own fears at bay.

"Tell you what. Let's finish the dishes and cleaning up. Then we'll make some dinner and we'll take some to Mom. You'll see that Mom is doing fine."

Daisy thought that was a good idea and feeling a little more comforted she picked up the cloth dish rag and began washing a bowl. She placed it in the empty pan to drip. Ellen also needed the reassurance that seeing her mom would give her so she lost no time. She washed the sticky jam off of the table, wiped the dripped porridge off the stove and swept the floor. Then she rinsed the cleaned dishes with hot water from the reservoir in the stove and Daisy dried them.

Ellen found some canned venison and tomatoes on a shelf in the pantry. She half-filled the large stew pot with water and placed it on the stove. The rubber seals on the glass jars gave a small crack when Ellen lifted them off with the metal opener. She paused a moment remembering the much louder cracks the rotten ice made in the river.

Added to the stew were potatoes, carrots and onions. When the stew started to simmer Ellen shook some salt and pepper into it, then watched the grains swirl around in a circular motion as she stirred it with a wooden spoon.

"Don't put so much salt and pepper in it," came the loud voice from behind her.

Ellen jumped and then gritted her teeth. She didn't respond to Mrs. Vanders command. Ellen felt perfectly capable of making the venison stew exactly the way her mom had taught her to.

"Is that milk cold and fresh?" Mrs. Vanders questioned while pointing to the jar of milk sitting on the counter.

"It's been stored in the well. I think it was put down there only yesterday," Ellen responded.

"Well, we don't want sour milk, do we?"

"It's not sour," retorted Ellen.

Mrs. Vanders wrapped her large puffy hands around the jar while muttering to herself. Then she went to the water bucket and scooped out a cup to take upstairs for Mom.

"I expect you know how to make a cup of tea?" said Mrs. Vanders.

"Yes, I can make tea."

"I'd like tea with my dinner then. Do you know how to make it correctly?"

"Yes, I think so."

"Make sure that the water is boiling hard before you put it into the teapot. You can't make good tea unless the water is boiling hard. Then you let it steep for at least four minutes. That's four minutes, do you understand? Oh, and make sure that you keep it warm. I can't abide cold tea."

Mrs. Vanders took a sip of water, arched one eyebrow, then said,

"This water isn't very fresh. It's warm and stale and look how cloudy it is. It needs to be fresh. Grab that bucket over there and go and pump some fresh water, girl. You can't make tea with that."

Ellen and Daisy exchanged a secret look of disgust but didn't respond.

From upstairs came the sound of Mom's crying out and Mrs. Vanders rushed down the hallway and up the stairs to attend to her.

Ellen's shoulders drooped as she looked at the water bucket that sat beside the sink. She scowled and muttered to herself,

"This water will have to do for her tea."

A few minutes later the water was bubbling in the large black kettle at the back of their stove. Ellen lowered the heat on the stew and poured hot water into her mom's teapot with the tea leaves and placed a kitchen towel around it to keep it warm.

I think Mom would like a cup of tea too, Ellen thought.

Daisy set the table while Ellen started to slice the half a loaf of bread she found on the pantry shelf. Then she spread creamy yellow butter and bright red saskatoon jam on the sliced bread to make sandwiches.

William appeared through the kitchen door with a basket of white and brown eggs and placed them close to the dish pan for washing later.

"Come and eat," Ellen said.

While William and Daisy were eating Ellen filled a tray lined with a red checkered tea cloth for her mom. The stew was hot and fragrant and the tea was just the way her mom liked it with cream and a wee bit of sugar in it. She was met at the top of the stairs by Mrs. Vanders who had just come out of Mom's bedroom.

"Your mom isn't hungry," she snapped.

"I think my mom should decide," answered Ellen. Then she added,

"Your dinner is waiting downstairs in the kitchen, Mrs. Vanders."

"Good. I see that the tea is nice and hot. That's good," said Mrs. Vanders after she felt the outside of Mom's teacup.

"Okay, then," Mrs. Vanders said and she opened the bedroom door allowing Ellen to slip in carrying the tray in front of her.

Her mom's pale face was framed by her long hair spread out on her pillow. She was tucked into bed with her favourite crazy work quilt that Grandma had made many years ago. One of her arms was wrapped around the mound in her middle.

"Come here, Ellen. Let me give you a hug."

Ellen put her tray down and happily wrapped her arms around her shoulders and snuggled into her neck. It was a great relief to see her mom and feel her warmth. She could hear her mom's shallow breaths and feel the sweat on her damp forehead.

"Mom, are you okay?"

"Ellen, everything will turn out fine. Soon we will have a new little baby sister or brother in the family. Won't that be exciting?"

Mom took Ellen by the hand and gave it a squeeze.

"You're a good girl, Ellen. Thanks for bringing me some tea."

"It's just the way you like it. Here let me put it beside you on the night table."

Mom looked up to see two more young faces peering at her from the bedroom door.

"Come in you two," she said.

They quietly inched their way in and stood staring at their mom. A strange look passed over Mom's face as she tried to suppress the new wave of pain that travelled through her body.

"Now children, best you go downstairs. I'll take care of your mom," said the coarse voice from behind William and Daisy.

With her massive arms she guided them all out. They looked back and heard a click as she firmly shut the bedroom door behind them. Once downstairs, they were aware of Mrs. Vander's heavy shuffles on the floor upstairs and their mom's occasional groans.

The chores outdoors still had to be done. Ellen milked the cows while William fed and watered the animals. Ellen was carrying a bucket of warm frothy milk that was sloshing back and forth in time to her steps towards the house when she heard the sound of galloping horses in the distance. She stopped and listened, then put the pail down and watched the dark figure travelling towards her on the gravel road.

"Dad!" she exclaimed.

Ellen was relieved to see her dad galloping on Nell towards her. Behind him moving just as quickly was Dr. Albertson in his horse drawn buggy.

After she quickly walked to the house with the evening's milk, Ellen put the pail in the kitchen beside the separator then went back outside.

"William, take care of the horses," she heard her dad say as he and Dr. Albertson approached the house.

"Dad, I'm so glad you're here."

Dad's breathing was rapid and his expression was worried when he said,

"Your mom. Is Mom all right?"

"Mom's okay, Dad. I just saw her."

Without wasting any more time he led Dr. Albertson into the house and up the dark stairs, disappearing into their bedroom.

After Ellen poured the milk through the separator, bottled the cream the way her mom always did it, cleaned the separator and got the milk ready to be stored down the well she joined William, and Daisy in the parlour to wait for news about Mom and the new baby. The air was silent except for a little quiet talk and the ticking clock on the mantle that obediently kept up with the eternal beat of time.

"How did you get across the rotten ice?" Ellen whispered to her Dad.

"Nell found our way across the narrow part of the river. Nell is smart. She knew where to go."

"Why did you go there?"

"It was faster, Ellen. Closer to our farm. Then when we came back we travelled further south down the river and came back across on the bridge."

"Do you think Dr. Albertson can help Mom?"

"Hope so. In fact, I'm sure he can so don't worry."

Then Dad closed his eyes, lost in his own thoughts. After what seemed like hours it came. They heard the bedroom door open, footsteps and then the tiny call of a baby crying. Dad raced up the stairs to greet his new baby son. When Dad returned, his eyes were lit up with joy and he said from the parlour doorway,

"Children, your mom is doing well and you have a new little brother."

"What are we going to name him?" said William.

"Do you have a favourite name?" said Dad.

"Thomas!" piped up Daisy.

"Thomas sounds good but I think we should name him after Grandpa," said Ellen.

William thought for a moment, then said,

"I like the name Thomas too, but couldn't we give him both names?"

"Okay, how does Thomas Edward Graham sound?"

They all nodded and then Daisy said,

"Can we call him Tommy for short?"

"I'll talk to Mom and see what she says," said Dad.

"When can we see the baby?" said Ellen.

Just then Mrs. Vanders entered the parlour with a tiny bundle wrapped in a yellow kitten soft blanket cradled in her arms. The children gathered around her but Mrs. Vanders pulled the bundle away from them.

"I want to hold him," said Ellen.

"No, I don't think you should. Children should stay in their places," said the coarse voice that was wearing a dough and sweat stained pink printed dress.

Ellen's eyes narrowed and she frowned as she gave William a hidden glance to one side.

"Don't worry, Ellen. I've got plans for the old biddy," whispered William.

Mrs. Vanders hustled the little infant out of the parlour door and back up the stairs without even allowing the children to have a good look at their new little brother. William and Ellen both looked at their dad for help.

"We want to see the baby," they both declared.

"Wait a minute," said Dad.

Dad followed Mrs. Vanders path and returned with the little bundle that was so tiny it nearly disappeared in the blanket that was tightly tucked around him. The three children gathered around him. His eyes that were lined with dark eyelashes were squeezed shut in his chubby face. He had a swirling crown of dark hair that framed his reddened pixie like features. His little fists were clenched and drawn up to his chin. Ellen touched his soft forehead with her finger and inhaled the fresh baby fragrance that was special to infants.

"Sit down here and I'll let you hold him," said Dad.

There was a stirring in her chest as she held out her arms and carefully snuggled him close in her cradled arms. She thought he was the most beautiful thing she had ever seen. She silently promised herself that she would be the best big sister ever and that she would be a better daughter by working hard to help her mom.

"My turn," said Daisy, and she sat down on the sofa and opened her arms to hold her new little baby brother. Her eyes were rapturous when Ellen carefully laid him in her arms, supported in her lap. He was not like Molly. He stirred, puckered his little lips and his eyelids fluttered until his dark eyes opened and looked right at Daisy. His brow creased into a frown then he shut his eyes tight again.

Mine, she thought. He's really ours.

"Okay, William. Your turn," said Dad.

William smiled in awkward fascination when he examined the little fellow in his arms.

Tommy, he thought. I wonder how long it'll be before I can take him fishing? His hair is as soft as my furry little chicks when they're born, he thought as he gently caressed Tommy's hair.

"I'll take him now," said the coarse voice from behind William.

"That won't be necessary," said Dad. "Mrs. Vanders, I want to thank you for coming and for all of your help."

"Really, Mr. Graham. Unruly children should be kept away from newborn babies. You never know what kind of germs they're carrying. It's been my experience..."

"Thank you again, Mrs. Vanders. We can manage now," Dad interrupted.

"But I always look after the newborn child," said Mrs. Vanders.

"Mrs. Vanders, we appreciate your help but we can manage now. There's no need for you to stay any longer."

"Well! In that case, you, girl... Go get my bag upstairs, and boy, hustle outside and hitch up my horse to my wagon. Make it snappy will you, and I'll be on my way."

"I should be on my way too," said Dr. Albertson appearing at the parlour doorway. "Congratulations all of you. You have a beautiful baby there. Kate is resting well and everything appears to be normal. If you have any problems, Billy, let me know, but I'm sure you won't need to."

"Thanks," said Dad, as he followed the doctor out the front door.

Mrs. Vanders climbed into her coat but left the buttons undone, then slapped her green hat on the top of her frowning and disapproving face. William hurried out to hitch up Mrs. Vander's horse while Ellen returned Tommy to his little bassinet beside Mom's bed and then carried Mrs. Vander's bag outside to her wagon.

Still frowning, Mrs. Vanders didn't acknowledge William and Ellen when they said goodbye to her. She just climbed into the wagon and sharply flicked the reins with a loud "Giddap!"

"Watch this," whispered William poking Ellen.

Ellen and William dissolved into giggles when they heard a blood curdling scream from Mrs. Vander's mouth. She stopped the horse and with her arms flailing about she jumped out of her wagon so quickly she almost slipped and fell while at the same time an unsuspecting green garter snake went flying through the air from out of the wagon. William and Ellen tried to hide their laughter as they watched her straighten her coat, reposition her hat on her head, then climb back into the wagon, and once more head down the road towards her home.

That evening, Nell got an additional helping of oats with some carrots and an extra long grooming from Ellen. As Ellen curried her coat until it was glossy she talked to her,

"We have a new baby brother. His name is Tommy. He's the most beautiful baby in the world and he's all ours. He's pretty small right now but you'll love him when he gets bigger. Good job today, Nell. We love you."

Chapter 12
Family Ties

Like a snake shedding its skin, the river discarded its winter coat of ice. As the now free flowing water rushed past, it was purged of debris and wreckage that had been frozen and still in the quiet tomb of ice and snow. There were branches, trees, parts of buildings and even dead horses that were swept away, cleansed from the fresh new spring flow of rushing water.

Daisy sat daydreaming in the sun-soaked grassy field just beyond the horse barn. Her world was blossoming with new little things. The generous sun was a spark that ignited and liberated the warming earth. Her new little brother, Tommy, was one of those small things. Even though Daisy loved him, she couldn't help but feel a twinge of regret that she was no longer the baby of the family. She thought as she chewed on a piece of grass, I bet Mom doesn't even know I'm out here. She's so busy with the baby.

A meadowlark carrying a small twig in her beak, hesitated on a fence post, then hurriedly soared to her nest in a nearby yellow green leafed balsam poplar tree. The swaying fingers of prairie grasses were stretching, growing and reaching up towards the energetic sun and the new warmth was pulled, and then absorbed into the busy ground at its feet. Daisy watched as a tiny black ant scurried up the grass stalk. Then she picked a blade of grass and slowly spread it apart. William told her she could make a noise with the grass by holding it between her hands and blowing on it, but try as she might, it wouldn't work for her, so she left it lying beside her on the ground. She was fascinated, drawn like a magnet to the springtime miracles that were all around her.

She remembered the soft yellow fluffy chicks that hatched over the weekend. The mother hen scolded William and Daisy when they pushed aside the feathers on her rump to see how many of the chicks had hatched. Scattered in the straw were pieces of shells and fuzzy yellow chicks, fluffing and shaking their tiny wings in blind confusion. They watched as one tender, almost transparent egg grew a longer and wider crack and then a tiny dark peephole where a tired miniature orange beak had pecked its way through the thin membrane and the shell into daylight.

William reached down and picked up one little chick. It fit right into the palm of Daisy's hand when he let her hold it. The chick tickled her hand with the fuzzy new down on top of its prickly feet and sharp pointed bill.

Just as Daisy was returning from her dreamy musings, her attention was drawn to a clucking and quacking somewhere beside her in the grass. A wild mallard mother duck was calling and instructing her newly hatched ducklings to follow her waddle to the tall reed bordered slough nearby. She was a protective light brown with a yellow bill and her little babies were yellow with a dark stripe down over their eyes and over their backs. Daisy watched, intrigued with the little black balls that popped up and down in the grass behind the mother duck.

With the mallard hen quacking and leading the way they followed her in a crooked line away through the grasses. When Daisy looked again, one little black fluffy duckling was left behind. It kept popping up and down, and peeping and as loud as it could, called for its oblivious mother. Soon the mother and her brood were nowhere to be seen. Only the remaining lonely little black duckling that jumped and peeped for its mother was visible.

That little duckling is in trouble. I think he's been left behind, and he's lost in the grass, thought Daisy.

Maybe I should help it. I think it needs a mother.

Daisy got up and quietly moved towards the panicked duckling. In its frenzy, the duckling didn't notice Daisy approaching. She bent over and gently contained the duckling in her cupped hands and cradling it in both of her hands she carried it back to the farmhouse. The duckling was quivering but remained quiet in the darkness Daisy created with her hand closed over its head. Even though Daisy entered the kitchen as quietly as she could, Mom heard the door open, felt the pools of fresh spring air and smelled the perfume of green grass and blossoms that followed Daisy into their kitchen.

Mom looked through the bedroom door from where she was sitting, tucked the baby blanket more securely around Tommy and said, "Daisy, what have you got in your hands? What are you bringing into the house?"

Daisy stopped and looked around through the doorway at her mom, her little charge still safe and quiet in her hands. She didn't respond to her mom's question.

Mom was seated on the bed with her back against a pillow resting on the wall. One leg was propped up on the bed while she was busy feeding Tommy. A shaft of sunlight fell in a column from the kitchen window and into the bedroom and like a sliver of moonlight it lit up and haloed the soft curls that framed her pretty round face.

She held Tommy across her chest. One arm supported his head that cuddled into her while the other one held his wrapped bottom. His eyes were closed in contentment as he suckled in satisfaction. His soft round head mirrored the smooth curves of Mom's bosom and pale arms that held her small child.

Daisy looked around and spotted an old cardboard box sitting beside their quiet wood stove. The box was badly worn with one flap nearly ripped off of it and the words *The Hudson Bay Co.* could plainly be read on the side of it. It still had splinters of firewood in it but Daisy thought that if she cleaned it out it would be a perfect home for her stray duckling. She held the wriggling duckling tightly with one hand and turned the box over with the other, emptying its bits and pieces of wood on the floor. The duckling dropped with a plop into the box. Once the little duckling was corralled it paced back and forth, bewildered at its surroundings. Daisy peered down at the frightened duckling, her long curvy ponytails reaching down nearly to the bottom of the box.

"Daisy, what have you got in there?" asked Mom from behind her.

Daisy had been so absorbed with her duckling she didn't notice Mom standing in the bedroom doorway watching her. She was buttoning up the front of her yellow printed dress as she spoke to

Daisy. Daisy had no choice but to show her what was inside the cardboard box.

"Mom, it's a baby duck. I found it when its mother left it behind."

"Oh, Daisy. It's a wild thing. You can't keep it in here."

"Mom, it's scared. I'll look after it. Maybe it can grow up and live with the chickens."

"Daisy, it really needs to be in the wild where it belongs."

"But, it's lost and I can take care of it."

"Don't argue with me. It needs to be outside where it was born."

"But, it'll die! I know it'll die."

"After you take the duck outside again, you'll have to clean up the mess on the floor."

Daisy's face grew long with disappointment.

Just then Tommy's cry could be heard and Mom rushed to tend to him. Daisy peered down at the ebony eyes looking at her from the depths of the box. The eyes were glassy and fearful. She couldn't bear the thought of this beautiful little duckling dying all by itself outdoors. In defiance she thought, I have to keep it. Mom doesn't even have to know about it. "Don't worry little duck. I'll take care of you. You'll see."

The little duckling jumped and beat itself against the sides of the box all the while peeping as loud as it could. It made a terrific display of terror by flapping its little wings against the sides of the box and pecking the cardboard with its small beak as it continued its struggle for freedom.

"I know what you need," said Daisy. "You need something to eat. Then you'll be happy. Maybe you're thirsty too."

Daisy tried to imagine what the duckling would eat. She knew that the chickens ate chicken feed, kitchen scraps and peelings from the compost.

The little duckling, ignorant of Daisy's pleas, simply repeated its tempestuous battle in its quarantined state.

Daisy closed up the lid of the box. She was so completely absorbed in her quest to mother the duckling that she was heedless of its fear. All she could think of was her duckling growing up and following her around the farmyard. She thought, I'll be its mother. I can take care of it.

Mom was still busy with Tommy, and Daisy was sure she could sneak away unseen with the duckling in the box.

I can't leave it here. Mom will make me take it outside. I know what. I'll take it upstairs to my bedroom. Ellen and William will know what to do with it.

Daisy tiptoed upstairs carrying the box. The box was bumping with the scratching and peeping duckling inside.

"Shhh," whispered Daisy. "We don't want Mom to hear you."

Daisy was able to successfully avoid her mom's scrutiny and sneak into her and Ellen's bedroom. She put the box down on the floor beside their bed, then sat down cross legged and peered inside. The little duckling cowered from her and she was alarmed to see that the duckling was panting both with fear and effort. Daisy thought, I need to find William or Ellen. They'll know how to look after you.

William and Dad were at the river bank having a great day bringing in the pickerel that were so plentiful in the rushing spring river. The sparkling water quivered in the sunlight while the busy black orchard bees hummed and darted about, searching for a winter nesting place.

Like a prism refracting colours in the sunlight, the fish were flashes of sparkly silver and rainbow colours of pink, blue and green, as they flipped and jumped in the cold spring river water.

"Hang on to the net. There, that's a big one. Nice and silver too," said Dad.

Dad and William used long handled nets to catch and bring the fish onto the shore. William grabbed the slippery gummy pickerel from out of the net and held it in his hands up to his face. Boy and wriggling fish looked at each other eyeball to eyeball until the pickerel gave a last flip, its dark eyes turning blank.

With a wicker basket that was overflowing with fish strapped over Dad's shoulder, their jackets over their arms, and carrying their nets, William and Dad walked down the gravel road to home satisfied with their Saturday morning outing.

At home, Ellen was busy finishing morning chores in the barns. She was busy pitching some clean hay in the horse stalls when she looked up and met the dark beady eyes and Cheshire cat grin on Mr. Beettle's face.

"What do you want?" said Ellen frowning at him.

"I'm here to see your father," he stated.

"He's not here right now."

Mr. Beettle was indifferent to Ellen's dismissive tone. He continued to try to engage Ellen in conversation.

"That's a nice horse I've seen you riding."

Ellen's eyes narrowed in suspicion. She didn't like Mr. Beettle, especially since he'd shown an interest in Nell.

"I don't know what you want, but my dad isn't here so you might as well leave."

"Leave! Hardly. Your dad and I have some business to talk over."

Mr. Beetle's fat fleshy face housed his dark eyes that held a smug glint and his gleaming perfect white teeth lined up in a row inside his smiling mouth. He scratched at the stubble on his face then answered,

"I'm not going anywhere until I talk to your father."

"If you think you're going to buy Nell, you're wrong. Dad will never sell her to you."

"Listen here little lady. Your dad will make that decision, not you."

"Ellen, that's enough. I think you should go back to the house," said Dad when he unexpectedly appeared from the shadows behind Mr. Beetle.

"But, Dad!"

"The house!" Dad said much more firmly.

Ellen's grip on the pitch fork tightened, the steel cold in her hands, until she reluctantly relaxed allowing the handle to slide down to the ground. Her shoulders sagged but her inflexible determination was still written in the cold stare she gave to Mr. Beetle and her tightly drawn lips that were frozen in silent protest. She gave both her dad and Mr. Beetle a mulish look, then threw the pitchfork down and stomped towards the barn door.

Mr. Beetle's unscrupulous smile never left his corpulent face as he watched Ellen leave, then he turned his attention back to Dad.

"We really don't want to sell Nell," said Dad.

"Oh well, you know everything has a price and I'm willing to make you a very generous offer, one I know you can't afford to turn down."

Dad scratched his head as though it would stimulate a happier solution to the family's problem. He'd weighed the options many times, taking into consideration his daughter's attachment to Nell. But the certainty of losing their farm to auction to pay for back taxes weighed like a ton of stone. In his heart and in the pit of his stomach he hated to face what he knew was the inevitable solution to their financial dilemma. They needed their home and the livelihood it provided.

"Let's talk outside," said Dad.

"Sure," said Mr. Beettle.

Mr. Beettle followed Dad out of the blue and purple shadowed barn into the bright golden sunshine and around to the back pasture where Sal was grazing.

"Have you had a good look at Sal here?" said Dad.

"She's got a much better temperament. She's strong, fast and intelligent. I'd be willing to sell her to you instead of Nell."

Sal's eyes followed Mr. Beettle, her ears twitching forward as they inspected each other.

"She's in good shape all right," said Mr. Beettle.

He drew a long breath while he mused, rolled his tongue out of the corner of his mouth and turned over the toothpick he was chewing as he thought for a moment then shook his head and said, "I'm sorry, Billy but it's Nell I came for. I really don't want Sal. She's older than Nell, doesn't have near as much wind and energy."

"Why don't you try riding Sal. She's got lots of strength left in her."

Mr. Beettle's sly smile and sleazy gaze slid from Sal over to Dad while he considered his proposal.

"Nope, but I would like to ride Nell. Now that one's got lots of spirit in her. I imagine she could run like the wind," Mr. Beettle said as he started to walk to the next field where Nell was standing, and Dad, looking quite dejected, followed behind him.

Nell looked up from her lazy grazing and stared at the two of them as they approached her. Her ears twitched forwards then back again in curiosity before she lifted her head and loudly bellowed a scorning and mocking neigh. Dad noticed some movement behind Nell.

"I thought I told you to go to the house," said Dad to Ellen, who was hiding behind Nell. Ellen had been whispering in Nell's ear that she should be wary of this horrible man because he wanted to take her away from the people that loved her.

Ellen stepped out from behind Nell, and with a scowl that would kill a bear, she stomped down the path towards the house. She slammed through the kitchen door, leaving the screen door swinging erratically until it rested wide open against the outer wall. Dishes rattled when the sudden jarring almost knocked down some recently washed cups and saucers that were sitting on the edge of the counter.

"Take it easy," said Mom from the room off of the kitchen.

"Why should I take it easy? Do you know what Dad is going to do? He's going to sell Nell to that greasy Mr. Beettle. I can't believe you and Dad would do that."

"He doesn't want to, but we need the money to pay the taxes," pleaded Mom.

"Nell is part of the family. Would you sell me or William or Daisy?" wailed Ellen.

"Ellen, listen. It's not something we want to do but sometimes we have to make difficult decisions."

"There has to be another way," screamed Ellen and she bolted from the kitchen into the parlour and threw herself down on the sofa. The blue cushions sagged and absorbed Ellen's frustrated tears.

Mom answered in a small, shaky voice, "Oh, please don't cry, Ellen. We'll get you another horse when things get a little bit better."

"I don't want another horse. There'll never be another horse like Nell. Mom, you and Dad can't do this!"

Mom looked through the doorway at her daughter crying as though her heart was broken. Her frown deepened over her eyes and she wondered if Ellen would ever forgive them. She felt wretched and honestly didn't know what else to say to Ellen. She hadn't ever minded the scarcity of money. Being poor was something she'd never thought of, as long as there was enough food to eat and their farm to provide a home for them all, but sometimes it was overwhelming and downright depressing when there just wasn't enough money to keep their home and pay their bills.

"Oh, Nell. What will happen to you?" Ellen cried into the pillows.

The kitchen door banged as it flew open and was followed by the sound of rushing footsteps.

"Ellen, come quick. You gotta see this," said William, as he came bursting down the hallway and into the parlour. His face was lit up like fireworks popping in the night air.

"I don't want to see anything," said Ellen stubbornly.

"No, Ellen. You gotta come. This is the best thing I've seen yet."

"What is?" said Ellen.

"Mr. Beettle trying to ride Nell. You gotta see this," William said.

Ellen jumped off of the sofa and followed William outside. Daisy stopped to listen to their voices drifting upstairs. The duckling was forgotten for the moment and she ran downstairs and outside to see what the commotion was all about. They couldn't believe their eyes and ears when they lined up wide eyed and laughing outside of the fenced pasture where Nell was giving Mr. Beetle a ride that he would never forget. Amidst the shouts and whinnies he was hanging on for dear life on Nell's back while she kicked and bucked in her effort to rid herself of him. The thunder Nell's hooves created echoed and mixed with the family's laughter.

"Whoa, you stupid horse," Mr. Beetle shouted. "Whoa, I say!"

His reddened face was puffed and heavy with exertion. The rolls around his midriff jiggled in time to Nell's bounces and the buttons that were already stretched at his middle were beginning to pop open. His hat bumped up and down on his sweating head until it finally sailed through the air, landing in a muddy puddle leaving his greying hair flying outwards in time to the vaulting horse.

Mr. Beetle was able to hang on to the reins and remained seated in the saddle even though Nell was turning around and around in circles, bucking, jerking and jumping.

Nell wasn't defeated. Fully in charge, she galloped completely around the field with a frightened Mr. Beetle just barely hanging on and returned back past the barn where she stopped suddenly, reared fiercely, and with one mighty buck she threw Mr. Beetle clear over the fence and straight into the dark green slimy pig manure pile that had only recently been shoveled there. In the contest between man and horse Nell was a clear winner.

Mr. Beetle landed head first and began immediately scrambling and blindly searching around in the muck. He sat up and with a sweep of his hand wiped the brown green sloppy poop from his eyes until first one eyeball was showing, and then dug the filth from the other eye. He blinked a few times until his vision was refocused. His stringy hair stood straight up from his head solidified by the sticky stools. Only the whites of his eyes showed through the greasy hairy animal dung that stuck to his face, invaded his nostrils and emphasized his wrinkled and puckered mouth. Some of the pig pies rose up in patches that stuck to his neck and shoulders.

"At least he had a soft landing," snickered William pinching his nose.

"What's he looking for?" said Ellen when she could find a breath between gales of laughter.

Her question was answered when Mr. Beetle looked up and sputtered through his gummy toothless mouth. Nell's sudden jerk and Mr. Beettle's swift ride over the fence had popped his new false teeth right out of his mouth into the pile of fresh manure. What a sight Mr. Beettle was, as he dug and searched for his teeth until he finally held them up. He sat back and looked at them with disbelief written on his shocked and sickened face.

"I wonder if Nell has enough spirit for him," chuckled Dad.

"He'll have to pick the dung out of his teeth. He'll need an extra big toothpick," said Ellen giggling uncontrollably.

Mr. Beettle held up his soiled teeth and muttered an indiscernible curse under his breath. As he started to get up his feet nearly slipped out from underneath him because the ground was slick with the moist foil waste. He glared at Nell who was standing nonchalantly on the other side of the fence looking quite innocent of any wrongdoing. She just gave her head a shake, made a soft whinny that suggested a snicker and started to munch on some green grass. The pigs who had been watching the drama from the edge of their pen snorted and grunted to each other. It seemed as if even their snouts were curled up in a mocking grin.

"Don't forget your hat," said Mom and she dissolved into giggles once more.

"You'll be sorry," Mr. Beetle mouthed through sputters.

He found his footing and stood up, his large smelly dark shape moved towards Dad.

"You'll regret it," he shouted louder, shaking his free fist in the air. "That horse is a demon. A demon I say!"

"Does this mean you changed your mind about buying Nell?" chuckled Dad.

"I wouldn't pay two cents for that demon horse! You'll regret it, Billy Graham. You'll all be out in the cold," he shouted.

They all just laughed louder. They just couldn't stop. Mr. Beetle retrieved his hat, brushed it on his pants, perched it on the top of his defiled head and gave it a good pat down before he turned and marched to his wagon. As he drove down the gravel road retreating towards his home, the smelly Mr. Beetle could still be heard shouting obscenities into the air.

Just as the Graham family neared the kitchen door, Mom heard Tommy cry and she rushed indoors to look after him. Tommy's cry reminded Daisy that she had left her duckling upstairs in its box. She could hear a faint peeping when she entered the kitchen and not wanting to be found out she rushed upstairs to try to subdue it.

"What have you got in there?" asked William from behind Daisy.

"Shhh. Don't let Mom hear you," said Daisy.

"Why? What are you doing?"

"I'll show you, but you can't tell Mom," said Daisy. "She'll make me take it outside."

Daisy opened the flaps on the top of the box and William looked at the desperate little duckling. It was tiring out and panting from beating itself against the sides of the box and peeping for its mother.

"Daisy, it'll die in there. It needs to be with its mother."

"But, its mother left it behind and it doesn't know where she is. Anyway, I want to keep it."

"You can't, Daisy. It needs to be in water. You don't know how to be its mother."

"Oh. What can we do?"

"I have an idea. You wait here. Don't do anything until I get back."

William ran down the stairs and out the door. It wasn't very long before he returned upstairs almost out of breath from running.

"I found it. Daisy, I found its mother. They're in the pond, swimming around where the cows like to drink just beyond the back pasture. Give me the duckling and I'll take it there."

Daisy reluctantly agreed and William carefully cupped the frightened little duckling in his hands and as fast as he could he raced outside and down the pathway to the pasture. Daisy watched from the back door. In spite of her disappointment she was relieved with William's rescue attempt.

Before too long William returned. He was puffing from his hasty mission.

"You should have seen it, Daisy. The mother duck and her ducklings were swimming on the other side of the pond and the duckling started to peep when it saw its mother. It almost jumped right out of my hand it was so happy. I put the duckling in the water and it swam across the pond. The mother duck and her babies met the duckling and surrounded it, quacking and peeping. Daisy, the duckling is happy now. You don't need to worry about it anymore. It's with its family," said William.

Daisy looked down at the ground and thought for a moment. Then she sighed,

"I guess it needs to be where it was born to be.

It's happier when it's with other ducks."

"Never mind, Daisy. You can help me with my little chicks. They're almost as cute as the duckling."

At William's invitation, Daisy followed him out to the chicken house to admire the new little chicks.

The farmhouse settled down in relieved contentment with everything the way it should be. Nell was in the home she belonged in and the now joyous duckling was reunited with its family. Now they knew that whatever happened, their greatest strength and source of happiness could be found in the family bonds that held them all together. Their future was uncertain but they could face it as long as they had each other. Their wealth lay in the love and loyalty of their family ties.

Chapter 13
Ellen's First Dance

The walls of the farmhouse kitchen chanted and vibrated with excitement like an ancient incantation invoking a spell, as they absorbed the musical rhythms that pulsated within it. Moving as one, the orchestra of Dad's tapping foot, the ticking clock, Mom's steady strong movements back and forth with the heavy iron, and Ellen's carefully measured strumming on her guitar harmonized with the rhythmic flow of their heartbeats.

Mom stopped ironing momentarily and lifted the heavy iron from the fabric she was working on. She returned the first iron to the roaring wood stove, released the handle from it, and then left it on the stove to heat up again. She hooked the handle onto the second iron and carried it to her ironing board to complete the job of smoothing wrinkles and pressing new seams on the soft blue cotton dress she was sewing. The scent of steamy heat rising from the heavy steel searing the comfortable cotton rose up and mixed with the sweat that beaded on Mom's forehead, dampening her hair and the underarms of her blouse.

Mom held up the altered dress and examined it closely. The material felt smooth in her hands and she was pleased that the old seams had disappeared into the pliable fabric. The seams were smooth, straight and even. She couldn't see where the old seams had been when they were ripped out and reshaped to fit Ellen's slender form.

"Ellen, can you stop for a minute? I need you to try this on again. The hem needs to be measured."

Ellen stopped playing and put her guitar down. Dad, satisfied with their practice, followed by putting the bow and his violin into the black violin case that was sitting on the floor beside him.

"I'm going outside to check that fence that needs mending," said Dad as he headed towards the kitchen door.

"If you see William, tell him I need some help."

The door opened with a tell-tale squeak then shut firmly followed by the whimpering screen door as it swung back and forth outside.

Mom handed the blue dress to Ellen and without comment she quickly ran upstairs to try on Mom's handiwork. Ellen fastened the buttons that paced up the front of the bodice of her dress, then straightened the white collar. She frowned a little at the empty bulk in the front where her breasts should fill. Mom took the darts in as much as she could but Ellen still couldn't hide her flattened state.

"Honestly, when am I going to look grown up? Mom says that young ladies shouldn't show their figures but I sure do wish I had something to hide."

Ellen pulled a little at the long loose wavy curls in her hair, and frowning, thought, "I need to do something different with my hair. Something more, well, sophisticated. Miss Larson wears her hair in a chignon. I wonder how on earth she does it that way."

While looking at herself in the mirror, Ellen picked up a handful of her hair and held it up on the top of her head. Her hair had grown long and thick over the winter reaching past her shoulders and down her back.

Some of the modern young ladies get their hair cut short and then curl it with pin curls thought Ellen. I saw some girls with short curly hair in a magazine at the store when I went to get the mail. Those young ladies sure look pretty.

She shook her hair free and thought, "Mmm… Loose maybe, with a ribbon… Oh well, maybe Mom has some ideas.

She studied her face in the mirror. Ellen was losing the round wide-eyed look of a child. Her features were longer and more clearly defined.

I don't like my nose. Why couldn't my nose be smaller, like Mary's or Miss Larson's?

Interrupting Ellen's thoughts was Mom's voice calling, "Ellen, what are you doing up there? I need to get this done while Tommy is sleeping."

Ellen glanced down at the crease where the old hem used to be, and at the loose threads at the bottom of the dress, and then she hurried downstairs to the kitchen.

Mom mumbled with a dozen straight steel pins sticking out of her mouth and gestured to Ellen to stand on a chair she'd placed in the middle of the kitchen floor. In her sock feet, Ellen climbed up and stood on the wooden kitchen chair. Mom tucked up the bottom of the dress so that the length modestly covered to the middle of the calf of her legs ("a decent length," Mom said). She held it there then removed a pin from her mouth and pinned the edge of the dress to its underside. When Mom had three pins lined up and was happy with the result, she stood back and told Ellen to run upstairs and take the dress off so she could finish sewing it.

"Hey, Ellie. You look all girlie in that. I bet George will like it," said William as he breezed through on his way outdoors.

"I don't care what that pest George likes!" huffed Ellen, her cheeks colouring.

"Your dad wants you to help him outside," said Mom.

William, still chuckling, was already out the kitchen door and on his way to find Dad and help with the fence mending.

Later that evening, Ellen was busy in the parlour decorating a small cardboard box and lid to take to the dance. She pulled some shiny red and silver paper from a brown paper bag that was holding their used Christmas wrappings and ribbons. It rustled and sparkled catching the light as she smoothed the creases where the folds had been. Then she placed the glowing paper against the box to see if it would fit over it. It was a perfect fit. Ellen folded it carefully to cover the box and lid then pasted it down to hold it in place.

The saskatoon pie Mom made this morning would look good in Ellen's decorated box. She reached into the paper bag and pulled the rest of the colourful paper and ribbons out. A lacy silver bow caught her eye. It was bent and a bit wrinkled from being confined in the bag with the other wrappings. The bow was quickly awakened, fluffed up and smoothed, then given new life in the center of the box lid. Ellen held it up and thought that for sure it would fetch a good price at the auction tomorrow night.

"Is anything wrong?" asked Mom. "You've been quiet all through supper."

"No, Mom."

"Are you sure? You look very pretty in the new dress I'm sewing for you to wear to the box social. Don't you like it?"

Mom was sitting in the rocking chair hand sewing the hem of Ellen's new dress. The soft creaking sounds of the gentle rocking kept time with the motion of her busy hands rocking, stitching and pulling the thread through the edge of the dress hem.

"I like it fine. I'm just a little worried. That's all."

"About what? You look very nice and you've been practicing the chords on your guitar every spare moment you have. You'll sound just as good as you look. Anyways, your dad will be there beside you so it'll be easy."

Ellen put the box to one side and finally said,

"I know, Mom, and I'm not worried about playing my guitar. I just don't know if I could dance. Not that anybody will ask me, but in case they did I don't think I could do it."

Mom raised an eyebrow and stopped sewing for a few seconds as she became thoughtful. It never occurred to her that Ellen would be shy of dancing.

She knew that Ellen had never been to a dance before and of course she would feel awkward. She smiled inwardly, remembering her first dance, how hesitant and shy she had been.

"I have an idea," said Mom out loud.

As though he had been summoned by Mom's thoughts, Dad poked his head into the parlour doorway and said,

"What are you two ladies talking about?"

"We need a dance instructor here and since you are the best dancer around, I think our daughter needs a lesson. How about it?"

Dad's face relaxed into a grin and he winked at Ellen,

"Sure, let's try it right now."

"Thanks, Dad," said Ellen and she quickly stood up waiting for Dad's directions.

"Okay, well, let's see. What should we practice? You know, Ellen that dancing is like playing the guitar. The same rhythms apply only you're using your feet instead of your hands. Your feet keep the basic rhythm of the music that you're listening to. For example, if you're dancing to a waltz, it's a 3/4 time. Here let me show you. Watch my feet."

Dad then took a stride ahead with his left foot and with his right foot a smaller step and a small step again with his left while counting 1… 2… 3…

Then he strode ahead on his right foot, smaller steps with his left, then right.

"Your job is to follow the man's lead, so you'll step on the opposite feet."

Ellen studied her Dad's movements then tried to mimic them as he was showing her.

"Stand up straight now, eyes front. Don't look at the floor and don't forget to smile."

Dad held Ellen around her back with one hand and took her hand in his other hand and as elegant and graceful as a pair of trumpeter swans they were in perfect formation.

They waltzed around the parlour avoiding the furniture while Dad patiently counted out their steps. It didn't take long for Ellen to overcome her jerkiness and coordinate the basic time of the waltz with the movements of her feet. Then Dad taught her the steps to the Waltz Quadrille, the Two Step and a simple Schottische. Ellen's worried frown turned into a relaxed smile. Dancing was fun, especially with her dad.

"Remember your dance etiquette, Ellen. If someone asks you to dance then you politely accept and dance with him," said Mom.

That night, Ellen drifted off to sleep with dance patterns and rhythms mixed with songs she played on her guitar gaily bumping and drifting through her mind.

Saturday evening, Ellen and her dad arrived at the community center with many of their friends and neighbours coming from different directions and all talking and greeting each other as they entered the hall with their good wishes and brightly coloured boxes.

The community hall was glowing with welcome in the last rays of the evening's sunlight. The center of the wooden floor was empty and chairs were placed around its perimeter. The stage area was being set up around the piano for the band to play for the evening's eager dancers.

Ellen carried her guitar in its case with one hand and her decorated box that housed the pie in the other. After she put her guitar behind a chair at the stage area she looked around to see where the lunches went.

In the far corner was a table with a lacy white tablecloth on it and beside it was Mrs. Stuart with her box lunch talking to Miss Larson. There were some boxes already placed on the center of the table for later and a vase of yellow daffodils blended with the colourfully decorated boxes. Ellen hurried over and placed her boxed pie with the others. The aroma of fresh food seeped out from the packages but Ellen wasn't interested in food. The butterflies in her stomach fluttered in time with the tremors in her legs and she wondered if she would be able to perform the music with her dad, and if she would remember how to do the dances her dad had taught her.

Her thoughts were interrupted by the sounds of chairs scraping the floor, the low rumble of happy chatter and the violin being tuned for the opening songs. Ellen and Dad weren't playing until after a break so she had some time to gather up her courage, watch the other people dance, and listen to the music. This was all so new to her that she was very quiet while watching the guests file in and the band set up.

Ellen sat down at the side of the hall and hoped that somebody she knew would sit close by so she wouldn't feel so alone. A warm sunny glow surrounded a lovely looking young blonde lady when she entered the front door. Her hair was cut in the style Ellen admired in the magazine, short and curly and her slender but curvy figure filled out her pink and white fitted dress. Ellen watched her confident greetings to the young people around her.

That's Jeannine thought Ellen. She's Mary's older sister. She has to be at least eighteen. She's so beautiful. I wonder who cut her hair like that. Boy, has she got a good figure.

Ellen scrunched up her shoulders and crossed her arms in front of her in an effort to hide, and thought with heat rising in her cheeks, I don't know about this. Oh dear, maybe I should have stayed home.

Just then another group came through the doorway. This time it was a group of boys. Most appeared to be older than Ellen and in the center of the group was none other than George. His sandy blonde hair was combed and slicked back in the latest style framing his mischievous bright eyes and cocky half grin. Ellen immediately looked the other way pretending to be bored. A quick glance back and she realized that she didn't know all of them but recognized Alphonse, the French boy from across the river.

I remember him. He was in Grade 5 when I was starting school she thought.

Interrupting Ellen's thoughts and the happy chatter in the hall, the band started to play the evening's first dance. Ellen was drawn into the music as it filled the air and aroused her natural sense of rhythm. She couldn't stop the heels of her feet from tapping in time to the lively jig they were playing. Every once in a while she glanced over at George who was teasing and laughing with the other boys.

The jig ended with everyone including Ellen applauding the band. The musical group consisted of four people. Mrs. Saunders was playing the piano; her friend, Mr. Wallace, was playing the violin; Mr. Stuart was playing the guitar; and Mr. McCaulie was sitting on a stool, with his broken leg supported on a chair and his crutches by his side, playing the banjo.

Just then George strutted past her, his hands in his pockets, but he looked the other way, ignoring Ellen, choosing instead the safety of the huddle in the corner of the hall.

"What a goof," groaned Ellen, rolling her eyes.

The band started to play again. This time they played *"Waltz Across Texas,"* and everyone shuffled to find a partner for the popular waltz. Ellen tried to shrink down into her shoulders, too frightened to even talk to anyone.

"May I have this dance?" came a familiar voice beside Ellen.

Ellen looked up and into the handsome face of her smiling Dad. She gave him a grateful nod, then stood and took his hand. Away they danced around and around the hall. The walls blurred and she felt breathless with joy as they glided and turned past onlookers at the sides of the animated hall. She felt light as a feather floating in the breeze and the smile that was on her face spread throughout her whole body and right through her filling up her senses.

When the dance was over Dad guided her by the arm back to her chair and Ellen couldn't help but notice that the huddle in the corner had turned to watch her.

She barely sat down again when a pimply faced young man approached her and asked her to dance. Ellen hesitated, then remembered her mom's instruction on dance etiquette, so she stood and gave him her hand. He didn't bother to tell her what his name was and she was too nervous to ask. With a forward jerk he pulled her close, too close, to him when they started to dance, and Ellen's eyes popped wide open with surprise. This wasn't the gentle elegant hold her dad used when she danced with him. His grip was tight and strong and she couldn't escape the grazing of hard metal in the breast pocket of his red plaid shirt. When she glanced down she saw the top of a silver whiskey flask. She knew that some of the older boys liked to gather and drink alcohol before a dance. Her dad told her about it and warned her to stay away from boys like that. Nobody drank alcohol at her house. Her mom wouldn't allow it. He kept smiling at her releasing a breath, heavy and reeking with rye whiskey, into her face.

"Uh, I don't think I'm feeling very good," said Ellen after a tour around the hall in a quick two step.

"Oh, sure. It's just about finished anyway. Thanks for the dance."

"Yeah, thanks," said Ellen and she found her seat again.

She perked up when she heard Mr. Wallace call out to Dad and Ellen to come up front and play in the band with them. Grinning, Ellen took her place on the stage and placed the guitar on her lap. She looked at her dad who was putting the violin up to his chin, his bow raised. Keeping her eyes fixed on him they started to play a lively rendition of *"Turkey in the Straw,"* a polka that got a happy crowd up dancing, and the rest of the guests clapping in time to the music. Her youthful and energetic strumming vibrated and echoed through the hall with a cheerful vitality. It was one of Ellen's happiest moments, the sounds of the music, the excitement and the delighted response of the audience. She blended into the moment and totally forgot to be self conscious.

When she returned to her seat at the side of the hall she was still feeling a little euphoric from her success on the stage. In a loud voice, Mr. Wallace announced that this was the last dance before the lunches were to be auctioned to the highest bidders.

As the first notes of *"Red River Valley"* filled the air, Ellen glanced down to see a shaky hand extending an invitation to her. She looked up and there was George looking a little frightened but determined. He looked different than he usually did at school. His green cotton shirt that reflected the green in his eyes was tucked neatly into his jeans, and Ellen was aware of a thin fragrance of cologne when he was near.

With a half-smile out of the corner of her mouth and a shy sideways glance, she put her hand in his, and when Ellen stood to dance with him George's face broke into a victorious smile. For a few awkward seconds words disappeared. He couldn't even think of something to tease her about. George's first step in shoes that seemed too large for his still growing frame landed squarely on Ellen's foot. They both started to giggle, then started again, this time together and he held her in his arms while they danced a perky two step around the edge of the dance floor.

"Which box is yours?" George asked Ellen.

Ellen explained that her box was the one in the red and silver paper and that it contained a saskatoon pie.

There was some lively bidding on the lunches but after dueling with the pimple faced lad, George paid twenty cents for Ellen's pie. They sat and ate together, talking about school, horses and what they were going to do this summer.

"Are you going to school in the fall?" said George.

"I don't know what will happen. I wish I could though," Ellen replied.

"I think I'll have to work on the farm. My dad really needs the help," said George.

"I think my dad is packing up to go home now. This was fun, but don't get any ideas," said Ellen with a smile and a twinkle in her eyes.

George hesitated and was about to respond with a tease then changed his mind. Instead he said, "You're the best, Ellen."

Chapter 14
Working on Sunday

A shaft of early morning light beamed through the open doorway of the thick dusky coloured timbers in the large barn that among other things housed the family's supply of grain. A crown of light circled the heavy wooden barrels beside the wheat bin in the corner reflecting soft rosy blue and purple shadows that deepened into receding opaque darkness. The silver light bounced off the handles of the shovels and pitchforks that sat against the walls waiting to connect with human energy and fulfill their purpose of the day. They didn't know it was Sunday.

The sound of the grains splashed the spring air as they bounced and toppled into the wooden box in Dad's wagon, and his face was reddened and sweating in the heat of his own exertion and the warm sun. His rolled up sleeves revealed the hardened glistening muscles that flexed with effort as he shoveled the wheat into the box.

"Can't you do that tomorrow?" said a voice from behind Dad.

"I need to have this ready so I'll get an early start tomorrow morning."

"But, it's Sunday," said Mom.

"I know what day of the week it is," said Dad.

"I know, but if you get up early tomorrow morning you'd have time to load the wheat into the wagon before you leave."

Dad screwed his face up in annoyance. He didn't think there were any good reasons to waste a day sitting around when there was work that needed to be done. In late spring the work days on the farm were long, difficult and tiring. The early morning light was a call to rise, and with it came renewed energy that fuelled a frenzied busyness, a never ending labour that was necessary to keep the farm productive and growing. There was little time to spare for frivolous activities, except at Mom's insistence, on Sundays. She always said that Sunday should be a day of rest and family fun.

On one of those warm sunny Sunday mornings when the endless blue sky extended an invitation to relax and enjoy, Dad decided that he needed to get a head start on his trip to Holland the next day. He was taking the wheat to have it milled in the large strong stone mill that stood on the southern outskirts of the town.

"Kate, where are William and Ellen?"

"I'm not sure but I told them they didn't have any chores to do today because it's Sunday."

"I don't care if it's Sunday. I need some help right now."

Dad sucked in a breath and paused for a moment while he thought about it, then he said, "This won't take long. It's just a little job then we can all relax. Tell William to come and help for about half an hour or so."

"Just half an hour? I thought you had that plough to get ready to go too."

Dad's voice had an impatient edge to it as he replied,

"Will you stop worrying. I'll get things done before you know it."

"All right, if you're sure it's only for half an hour. Jenny Stuart said that a group of neighbours are getting together and she invited us to join them for a picnic and a visit. They're all meeting at the field beside the community hall this afternoon."

"First things first. Just see if you can find William, otherwise I'll have to do it all by myself and we'll never be able to go."

Dad resumed his shoveling, focused and totally absorbed in the job he was doing. Mom frowned, then reluctantly silent she turned to go back to the house to search for William.

Sunday afternoon dragged on. The half hour job stretched out with one task replacing another until the afternoon heat melted into the cooler air of early evening. The lazy afternoon outing that the family was supposed to enjoy didn't materialize. Instead, Dad felt a smug satisfaction at the work he'd been able to accomplish. The wheat was loaded into the wagon, the plough was repaired and loaded into the back of the wagon, its sharp teeth gleaming in the light. The barns were mucked out and the animals fed and watered. He even managed to get the gate to the pig's pen fixed. Everything was in order and Dad didn't understand the looks on the faces of his disappointed family. Nobody said a word. They didn't have to. Their glum looks told the whole story.

Monday morning rose early marked by the harsh shrill call of their white leghorn rooster. Mom rolled over to a cool soft empty impression in the bed where Dad slept. He was gone and as she opened her sleepy eyes she realized that he was already outside getting ready for his trip to Holland. Mom stretched a little, and lazily yawned, drawing in new air and shaking off the nocturnal cloak of drowsiness.

Her slow return to alertness was interrupted by a loud slam of the kitchen door, the sound of heavy boots pacing back and forth and the muffled male voice downstairs. Dad was in the kitchen and he didn't sound very happy. He was talking to himself and his words were bouncing and echoing off of the slumbering kitchen walls.

Is he cursing thought Mom. What on earth could be wrong?

Mom hurried downstairs to see what all the fuss was about.

"You haven't had breakfast yet," said Mom.

"I don't care about breakfast," Dad replied a little too loud.

"What's wrong? Why are you so upset?"

"That dang fool wagon wheel is broken. I just can't believe it. Just because I loaded it with the wheat and the plough."

Dad shook his head in irritation and half muttering he continued,

"I parked the wagon too close to the barn outside and the ground is uneven there. The load shifted to one side slanting towards the barn. Now the spokes are broken on the back wheel. The horses can't pull it."

"What are you going to do?"

"Fix it, I guess," growled Dad. "Now I've got to unload the wagon, take the wheel off and put another one on."

Mom tried to stifle a grin and resisted the urge to say, "It's your own fault for working on Sunday." Instead she said, "Isn't there an easier way to do it?"

"No, damn it. I wish there was."

"Well, never mind. Sit down and I'll make you some breakfast."

"No time for that. I've got to get going and change that wheel."

Ellen, William and Daisy passed the wide mouth of the barn door on their way to the road that led them to school. They could hear Dad filling the air with mutterings as he struggled and grunted with exertion. They didn't dare make any comments but watched briefly at the doorway. Dad was shoveling as though possessed, the grains flying into the barrels that stood outside the barn. The plough was sitting on the ground at the back of the wagon.

"Did you move that yourself?" asked William.

"Yes, and you three had better get a move on to school. Come on now. Off you go."

Two and a half hours later, after Dad fixed the crippled wagon and reloaded the wheat and the plough he was finally ready to hitch Sal and Nell to the wagon and head south down the road towards Holland. Mom had made some sandwiches and hot soup for him but when she tried to give them to him when he was heading out of the kitchen door he was in such a hurry that he replied,

"I'll be home before you know it. I don't need any lunch."

He was very late getting started on his journey. The sense of satisfaction he'd felt on Sunday was replaced on Monday by a heavy shadowy feeling that didn't lift once they started the fifteen mile ride to Holland. Dad flicked the reins urging Nell and Sal on with their heavy load. He wanted to drive the five miles to the ferry that would take them across the river as quickly as possible, and he hoped that he'd be lucky and wouldn't have to wait too long for passage across to the other side.

Dad drove up to the tiny ferry dock, reigned in the horses with a strong pull and he sighed with relief at the sight of the ferry sitting there waiting for its next passenger to take to the other side of the river.

"Hey there, Billy. Going to town today?" asked an approaching stout middle aged man.

"Yup, I gotta load of wheat to get milled. Had some trouble getting started this morning, so I'd appreciate a quick ride across."

"Well, you're in luck today. There's no one else using the ferry, so as soon as we get you loaded you can be on your way."

Albert MacDonald, who lived close by in the house by the river with his family, was the caretaker of the ferry. It was his job to maintain it and when travelers needed to get to the other side he would guide them onto the ferry and start the motor that would propel the small shuttle, guided by a cable, to the other side.

With Albert's assistance Sal and Nell gingerly stepped across the planks and onto the wooden platform while exchanging soft whinnies of encouragement to each other. Dad put the brakes on and jumped out of the wagon onto the floor of the ferry. He walked to the front and grabbed a tight hold of Nell and Sal's leather halter reins in his hands, speaking quietly to them. The sound of the motor starting up harmonized with the fast paced chorus of the tumbling water and with a wave goodbye to Albert, Dad and his wagon load was off on the next leg of his journey.

They were slowed down when they reached the slough hills, a series of three very steep hills. The gravel road travelled up, cresting the top of the hill and then down to the other side again. The horses had to walk and control the heavy load going up and down on the difficult terrain. On the last steep downhill grade Nell and Sal started to run gathering speed as they neared the bottom of the hill and the flats that lay wide open before them drawing them to their destination.

The sunny sparkle of the noonday sun disappeared behind a vast blanket of dove grey clouds. A quick look up at the sky told Dad that they were probably not rain clouds and would likely blow away. There was, however, a sharp cool heaviness to the air and an uncertainty about the ride home later. Dad was beginning to relax, his spirits rising, as he approached the town. If he didn't waste any time he could get the errands run and be back on the road home in a couple of hours. The plough he'd borrowed needed to be returned to the Johnsons' at the other end of town, not far from the large stone building where the wheat would be milled.

Nell and Sal trotted down the main street lined with friendly neat looking houses. They were outlined with short fences and well-tended spring flowers and bordered with small patches of green grass.

Out of the corner of his eye, Dad caught sight of a large red and white ball that bounced in front of his wagon and only in the nick of time he then saw a small girl on his right side dashing straight into his path to catch the ball. Dad pulled hard on his reins and shouted, "Whoa!"

The horses jerked to a stop but the wagon skidded to one side at the sudden termination of its motion.

The little girl stood frozen with fear directly in front of Nell and Sal. Her eyes that had been focused only on her ball were now looking straight at Dad, wide with disbelief. Dad climbed down from his seat on the wagon and approached her.

"Are you okay?"

The girl's lip trembled and her blonde curly pigtails, wrapped in blue ribbons that matched her blue plaid dress swayed back and forth in time to her affirmative nod. She was too shocked to move or say anything until a maternal voice was heard calling out to her in the distance. She recovered, ran across the street, through a swinging white gate and on through the front door of the painted white house.

Dad watched her go then walked to the back of the wagon to make sure that his load was still intact.

Oh, no, he thought.

His shoulders sagged and he took his hat off and scratched his head. He couldn't believe his eyes. The plough had fallen out of the back of the wagon. He kneeled down to have a closer look and to his dismay he discovered that the chisel of the plough had broken in the fall.

Now what am I going to do, he thought. I can't return it like that. Maybe they can help me at the blacksmith's shop.

For the third time this trip Dad had to reload the plough into the wagon. His energy was leaving him as he hauled one side of it and then the other back into place inside the wagon. He took the broken piece with him and climbed into the driver's seat. Before he started on his way again he looked up at a pale blue and white house on the left side of the road. He was sure he saw movement in the lace curtains that were held back in an upstairs window. With a shake of his head and a jerk on the reins he yelled, "Giddap!" and off they went down the main street of the town.

Dad turned right and drove past the colourful little shops and businesses all the way to the end of the street. There was no sign to identify it, but the blacksmith's shop was indicated by the heavy dark equipment seen through a wide open timbered doorway. The husky, darkly bearded blacksmith wearing a sooty apron blended into his shadowy surroundings. He looked up at Dad, his eyes questioning Dad's business with him.

"I've got a problem with my plough," explained Dad. "Its chisel is broken and I'm wondering if you can fix it for me."

"Leave it here and I might have time to work on it before the end of the week."

"The end of the week, eh? I need to return it to its owner today. Is there a chance that you can fix it today?"

"Today? I'm pretty busy. Well, let's have a look at it."

Dad handed the chisel to the blacksmith without saying another word. He hoped that it would be a small matter to fix the plough. The blacksmith turned the broken chisel in his rough blackened hands, then looked at the plough in the wagon.

"Ah, sure. It's a small job. I'll do it for you today. Come back in a couple of hours and it'll be ready."

Dad helped the blacksmith take the plough out of the wagon and after a grateful "Thank you," he started on his way again towards the mill house.

The large imposing grey granite building that housed the milling stones was five stories high and the walls were two feet thick. Dad pulled up as close as he could get to the entrance of the building, and went to get John, the miller, to help him with the wheat.

"How soon can you have the flour ready?" Dad asked.

"Well, let's see. What have you got there?"

"There's approximately 300 pounds of wheat to be milled."

"That'll make six sacks of flour, five for you and one for me. Once the wheat is milled and separated you'll have about four fifty-pound sacks of baking flour and one sack of bran. Does that sound about right?"

"Sure. Can you do it right away?"

"Soon as I get the stones started and the wheat into the steel bin."

Dad and John worked together to unload the wagon and as soon as the wheat started to trickle down between the large stones the gentle whirring of the turning wheels became a loud grinding groan. Dad's thoughts returned to the rejected lunch Mom had made for him. He was hungry as a bear, tired and needing a rest before heading back down the road towards home. Dad signaled to John that he would return and he went back outside of the vibrating building. He thought he would take the horses to the stables for some food and water. Then he might find something for himself.

"Is that your wagon there?" a deep commanding voice from a tall uniformed man standing at the back of Dad's wagon cut through the air. Dad blinked then tiredly frowned. He was looking straight into the chest of a towering police officer, then he looked up, found his voice and answered, "Yes, I just brought my wheat to have it milled into flour."

In a stern and strong voice the officer continued, "I see. Were you carrying anything else in your wagon?"

"I did have a plough that I had to return."

"What kind of a plough was it?"

"It was a pull plough. I borrowed it to till my fields before seeding grain on my farm."

"Where is it now?"

"It's at the blacksmith's shop. What's the problem, officer?"

It felt warm to Dad. His skin felt clammy and sticky inside his clothes even though the clouds were still shielding them from the sun. The officer looked cool and composed in his crisp uniform and regulation beige brimmed hat. He showed no emotion nor did he explain what his interest was in the plough, and continued, "I think I need to see the plough. Let's go to the blacksmith's shop right now."

"Why? Is something wrong?"

"Just follow me and we'll have a look at it."

Driving his wagon, Dad followed the RCMP officer on his dark horse and they pulled up in front of the shop where he'd left the plough to be repaired. Dad followed the officer in to talk to the blacksmith. With no food and nothing to drink for most of the day he seemed to be shrinking with frustration and fatigue as he stood next to the large and imposing figure of the investigating officer. He didn't think his day could get any worse than it already had and he sincerely wished it was over and he was back at home on the farm.

The hesitant blacksmith confirmed that Dad had brought the plough in to have it repaired, then noted to the officer,

"He insisted that it had to be repaired today. What seems to be the problem, officer? Should I fix it?"

"Oh, sure. Go ahead."

"Is the plough his?" asked the blacksmith.

"I'm not sure but we'll get to the bottom of this."

The officer turned to Dad and said, "My office is just down the street. I think we should have a talk about the plough. Just follow me."

Dad was tired and the sweat that beaded on his forehead wanted to drown the confusion of this exhausting day. He didn't understand what the problem with the plough was but he heaved a sigh and with a flick of the reins went with the officer and stopped in front of a small building sandwiched between a general store and a dry goods store. A large glass window looked into a sparsely furnished office. He saw a wooden desk in the center and a comfortable looking chair behind it. On entering the compact police station, Dad noted the tall wooden cabinet in the corner that he supposed held authorized police reports and there looking directly back at him on the opposite wall was the closed door that led to the jail behind it.

"You know, officer, I've been on the road for most of the day. My horses need some water."

"In good time. Now tell me where you got the plough. Is it yours?"

"No, it belongs to Mel Johnson. I borrowed it and I need to return it to him today."

The officer sat down and leaned back in his chair behind his uncluttered desk, then explained, "It was reported to me that you were seen stealing the plough just a short time ago."

"Stealing! How could I steal it? Who said that?"

If Dad thought he was tired before, it was nothing to the weariness he now felt. After giving the officer his name and where his farm was, he told the officer about the little girl chasing a ball that ran out in front of his wagon and that he nearly hit her but managed to stop in time. The plough had fallen out of the back of the wagon and he had to reload it. The chisel of the plough was broken so he'd taken it to the blacksmith's shop. Dad couldn't tell for sure but he thought he saw the officer's eyes soften and the beginning of a grin on his official face.

"I'll need to check it out with Mel Johnson but I don't see any need to write a report on this yet. Sit down and wait here while I go and talk to the Johnsons. I'll be right back."

Dad heard the officer's heavy boots stride to the office door and watched through the window as he mounted his horse and headed towards the Johnsons' house. Dad slouched in his chair, then took out his pocket watch to see what time it was. He groaned. The gold hands of the watch indicated that it was four o'clock, nearly supper time and soon the shops would be closed for the day. He needed to get back to pick up the broken plough and the flour in the next hour. He wanted to hurry but it felt to

Dad as if everything was moving in slow motion. In fact this day was dragging on and on, when all he wanted to do was to head for home. When the officer finally returned, he said to Dad, "You can go now. Someone just misunderstood what happened."

"Can I ask who reported this?"

"Uh, just a lady that lives on the main street. She's an elderly widow and I don't think she sees all that well. I guess she was watching from out of her window."

Dad just shook his head but managed to collect himself enough to say, "Thanks, officer. I'll be on my way now."

The plough was picked up from a suspicious blacksmith and returned to the Johnsons'. Then the sacks of flour were loaded into the box in the wagon and Dad's errands were finished. He was hungry and thirsty. The horses were hungry and thirsty too and he didn't think he'd make it all the way home without stopping for some nourishment, so he drove to the stables and watered and fed Nell and Sal.

With the cooler air of approaching evening came the "closed" signs dangling on some of the shop doors, shopkeepers who were busy locking up while others were already hurrying down the street towards their homes but the restaurant in the sociable looking hotel was still open and was serving dinner.

Dad stopped the horses and climbed out of the wagon. The street smells of horses and spring blossoms were infused with the savoury aroma of roasting beef. He was famished and the emptiness within him spread up his back and into his tightened face and tired aching eyes. His thoughts clung to a good supper of roast beef with all of the trimmings.

Once inside, he relaxed into a seat at a white covered table by the lacy curtained window and when a waitress approached him he asked her what the daily special was. The pretty young waitress smiled at him and said, "Roast beef with potatoes and gravy. There's apple pie for dessert as well."

"Good. I'll take that then. Will it be long? I need to be on my way soon."

"Not more than five minutes, sir," she replied and left to give the order to the cook.

Dad looked around at the other people in the dining room. Two unshaven men in grey worn and patched work clothes sat at one table and a stout lady wearing a yellow dress and a wide brimmed hat trimmed with fabric daisies dancing around it sat at another. Her chubby bare arms rested on a generous broad midriff that bulged against the edge of the table where she was sitting with her thin, gaunt looking, suited husband. Directly across from Dad were two young ladies happily chatting over their dessert of chocolate cake.

Dad was surprised to see that the patrons had stopped eating and talking and were staring right at him. He wondered what they found so interesting. He was just a tired farmer who needed to have something to eat before heading back home to his farm. Dad noticed his old friend, Leonard Bristol, walking towards him and he raised his weary hand in greeting.

"Hi there. How are you doing? I hear you had some trouble today."

"I've had better days. What'd you hear?"

"Well, that you've been in to see Officer Smith at the RCMP office."

At that the room went silent again as onlookers waited to hear Dad's explanation. Dad was too exhausted to relate the whole story so he simply said,

"It was nothing important. We got it all figured out."

In unison the dining room looked away from Dad and resumed eating.

After finishing his supper Dad paid for his meal and put his hat on, then left to start his journey home.

The grey clouds shrouded the setting sun and a cool breeze drifted through the edge of darkness that was settling on the wide horizon of the prairie. Dad was driving the last five miles towards home when he felt the moist coolness of raindrops on his face. It was a prelude to the explosion of heavy rainfall that descended down upon him. He was glad that his flour was hidden away in the covered boxes, protected from the rainfall but he shivered when the rain soaked right through his light coat and shirt. Rain dripped off of the brim of his hat and down his neck, its frigid fingers seemingly crawled through to his spent bones. The wet light shimmered off of Nell and Sal's muscular backs as they hurried towards their warm dry barn.

Once Nell and Sal were inside the barn and bedded down for the night, Dad plodded towards his darkened house. It was late and he supposed that everyone was already sleeping in their beds when he entered the kitchen door and crept upstairs. His thoughts of the frustrating day were suspended in the cool damp air, and with his teeth chattering like singing crickets, he searched for a warm spot under the comforting quilts of their bed.

Mom felt his coolness next to her and she turned to face him.

"Billy, you're home. You've had a long day. I hate to tell you but the government agent for the tax department was here today."

"Oh Lord! What next!"

"Billy," said Mom.

"Mmmmm," said a drowsy Dad.

"What would you like to do next Sunday?"

Chapter 15
Poison Ivy

"Ellen, can you come and help me for a few minutes?"

Mom was walking down the path that led to the cow pasture. In her arms she was carrying her constant companion, Tommy. He was wearing only a white cotton undershirt and a diaper exposing his chubby arms and legs. Mom's arm was wrapped around and tucked under his bumpy bottom and her other hand supported his soft and supple body. With his head nestled against her shoulder, eyes closed and his rosy lips puckered, he sighed in contentment with the soothing rhythms of Mom's heartbeat next to his.

"Ellen!" Mom called a little louder. "I need your help."

Ellen appeared from the open door of the barn. Dressed in a short sleeved blue blouse and jeans cut off above her knees, her golden tanned arms and legs and bare earthy feet were exposed. Her dark curly hair was tied back from her tanned and freckled face. She held one hand up over her clear radiant eyes that squinted into the sunshine.

"What's wrong, Mom?"

"Where's Dad and William?"

"They left together in the wagon. I think they were going to help the Stuarts with some planting."

Mom sighed with resignation and gave Tommy a shift to a more comfortable position on her chest, then said, "Some of the cattle got loose and have escaped to the school section in the muskeg. We need to chase them out of there. Come with me, Ellen and we'll try to herd them back home."

The "school section" was a parcel of land on which taxes were shared by the neighbours to financially support the school in the area. In one part of the section was a grassy bog. Like a wet sponge, the damp moist mossy earth of the muskeg supported clumps of stunted willow trees, pussy willows in occasional ponds and an abundance of yellow marigolds, violets, and pink lady slippers in the spring. The rich low growing plants and willows attracted animal life such as ducks, cranes and beavers that feasted on the willow bark and made their homes on the out flowing streams that fed the main artery of the Assiniboine River. The cattle loved to escape into the wet mushy land to graze on a variety of low growing plants. A particular favourite was the pea vine that grew in abundance in the marshy wetlands.

Mom, carrying Tommy, followed Ellen down the gravely path, then across the ditch and into the tall grass. The cool fresh grass tickled Ellen's bare feet as she led the way. She avoided the drying brown clumps of cow manure crowned with colonies of black flies circling over them and small white daisies sprouting from around their perimeters. The air was steamy with a melodic hum that buzzed and glowed in the sunshine and the casual conversation between Mom and Ellen.

"Next weekend is the community picnic," said Mom. "It should be fun this year."

"Is it on Sunday?"

"Yes, that's what is planned. I'm sure it'll be a nice day. Even though it's only June, the sky is clear and the air is very warm."

"Are they having races this year? Last year it was so funny when Mr. Peterson broke right through his gunny sack in the sack race. He just kept on running and finished holding the sack over his head. Oh, and remember when George's egg broke when it fell off of the spoon and he just picked it up and put it back on the spoon even though the yolk was dripping down the front of his shirt. I hope Daisy will go in the races this year. Last year she was too shy," said Ellen.

"Your dad is helping to organize the races. I think he's going to have one or two just for the young ones. I'm sure Daisy will try this year."

"Who is Dad going to run in the three legged race with this year?"

"I don't know. Not with me. I do enough running after children."

"Mom, are you bringing some watermelons to the picnic?"

"No, they won't be ready for another month or so."

"Oh, that's right. It's too early for them yet. You sure grow good watermelons. I'll bet they're bigger and juicier than anyone else's around here."

"I planted them according to the phases of the moon and everything is growing beautifully."

"Dad thinks that's silly."

"He does, does he? Well I'll have you know that lunar planting works very well. It's never let me down yet."

"What is lunar planting anyway?"

"I don't understand why it works but it has something to do with the moisture rising and falling in the soil. Something like the tides of the oceans.

Watermelons are planted two days before a full moon. Your grandfather always planted that way and he had wonderful crops, too."

Ellen stopped walking and looked straight ahead.

"There's one," said Ellen, pointing to a slow swishing tail behind a clump of trees that climbed a low rising hill out of the bog.

The cool moist water seeped through the saturated moss and squished Ellen's toes as she walked towards the runaway cow. Mom was right behind her, making her way to the stunted willows where the cow was hiding. Ellen sprinted ahead waving her arms and shouting, "Shoo! Get going. Go home!"

Mom followed Ellen up the hill and called to her, "There they are. The other two are over there."

Mom's eyes were straight ahead of her but as she rounded the stand of trees, in her haste, she almost tripped over a piece of wood that was nailed to a tree. Mom managed to find her balance by putting one hand on the tree trunk while hanging on to Tommy with the other arm. When she turned to inspect what had nearly caused her to fall she was amazed to see a large metal container braced with wood planks to the tree. It was joined with metal tubing to a tall metal container beside it. She peered into the first round tub and noticed it still had a residue of boiled mash on the sides of it. The tall container was empty but Mom knew that was where the steam was cooled off with ice, and as it cooled the steam dripped alcohol into the waiting jars.

She forgot the cows for a moment. As she circled the foreign metal contraption her questioning frown turned offended then indignant as she slowly realized that she was looking straight at a still. Its guilty metal body was hiding, obscure behind the willow trees in the bog.

"What's this thing doing here? Can you believe it? Someone was making moonshine, and on the school section too. Honestly, what some people will do."

After a thoughtful pause Mom continued, half to herself, "I bet it's that greasy good for nothing Ralph Beettle that's making it. That's how he can afford to buy things. He probably sells moonshine!"

"What is that?" questioned Ellen pointing at the strange looking piece of equipment.

"It's a still for making alcohol."

"I thought you weren't allowed to make alcohol."

"We're not! That's why it's hidden out here in the bog."

"What are you going to do?"

At that point Tommy started to wriggle and fuss.

It was feeding time and he was getting impatient. Mom shifted him again, feeling a wet spot in front that leaked through her dress. She said to Ellen, "I don't know. I guess I'll tell your dad and let him take care of it. Ellen, you'd better herd the cows back home. I need to get Tommy home and feed him. I'll see you back at the house."

Mom turned and without wasting any time she walked back to the farmhouse. As she retreated it was hard to tell if the steam that was rising from around her and Tommy came from the bog or from her angry state.

One by one the soft brown cows casually stopped their lazy chewing, the half-eaten green herbage still sitting in their mouths, and gazed a nonchalant question at Ellen when she waved her arms at them and shouted, "Shoo!"

With a jerky start, the cows started to make their way after Mom towards their own pasture at home. Following behind their waddle walked a daydreaming Ellen.

Only one more week of school. I'm glad to be finished with Grade 8, but it's going to be lonely without seeing my friends at school every day. I'm really going to miss my teacher. I wonder what city kids do when they finish Grade 8. I bet the schools there go all the way to Grade 12. Some kids are lucky. They can graduate while they live at home.

Ellen looked up and stopped to see if the cows were still following the path towards home, then resumed walking and thinking.

I wonder who was making the moonshine. Mom thinks it was Mr. Beettle. That sounds about right for him. Who would want to drink that stuff anyway? Ellen's focus shifted as she thought, Nell hasn't been out to pasture yet today. Pea vine. Nell would like some pea vine to eat. I'll just look for some to take to her.

Ellen stopped walking and watched the cows continue on their way, then looked around to see what was growing on the edge of the path. She wandered off to the left where the plants looked rich and succulent and started to search for the dark green leaves of the pea vine that all the animals loved to eat. She watched and then followed a monarch butterfly as it darted and fluttered its way through a jungle of low growing plants, and there right in the center of it was a trail of the coveted vine. Ellen moved towards it, and breaking it off with quick jerks, she gathered up an armful to take back to Nell. The bundle of pea vine felt cool and damp cradled in her arm. She was pleased with her treat for Nell and she knew that Nell would be too.

Ellen was almost home when she started to feel a tingling in her feet. At first she just ignored it but it felt like a hundred ants were marching up and down her legs and crawling all over her feet. When she stopped to look down at them she couldn't see anything unusual so she kept on walking. By the time she was back to the barn, her feet and lower legs were burning and red with itch.

Oh no, thought Ellen. What did I do? This doesn't feel like mosquito bites.

Ellen quickly dropped the pea vine into Nell's manger and headed for the house in search of Mom. The itching and burning on her feet and legs was very disturbing and seemed to be getting worse with every step. Ellen stopped every few yards to scratch and rub her ankles, with her eyes a frown of annoyance. The back door of the house was open and only the screen door was closed. Ellen could hear her parents' voices through the door and she stopped at the sound of Mom's voice.

"It's that Ralph Beettle that did it. I know it. Billy, you need to call the RCMP."

"Now, Kate. There are some things that should just be left alone," said Dad remembering his recent encounter with Officer Smith in Holland.

"I don't care. It's against the law."

Ellen wasn't sure but she thought she heard Dad chuckle as he replied, "Just forget it. Let them be if they want a drink or two. We have more urgent problems to worry about."

"The taxes," Mom said.

"Yes, those taxes," said Dad.

"What are we going to do?"

"I've talked to the auctioneer in Holland about selling our livestock and farm tools at auction. I'm hoping that we'll raise enough to pay the taxes."

"When will that happen?"

"In four weeks, so we'll have to get everything ready for selling by then."

"Will that give us enough time before the taxes are due?"

"Hope so. I also talked to the government tax agent and he says they'll stay the payment until after the auction."

"How will we manage next winter? How will we get our grain in?"

"We'll sell the livestock first and hopefully we'll get enough money from that and it won't be necessary to sell anything more. Trouble is, I don't know how much money people have to spend these days."

"It'll be hard to start over again without livestock but if it works at least we'll still have our home. Do you think the cattle will bring enough money to pay the taxes?"

"I don't know, but all we can do is try."

The conversation inside the house gave Ellen a jolt and she sat down on the cool grass outside the door, her head resting on her forearms as if it would relieve the shock. If Ellen thought the itching was disturbing, it was nothing compared with the thought that she still might lose Nell. She was dizzy with worry. Struggling to focus, she thought, Whatever will we do? Are they still going to sell Nell? What will happen to her? Ellen's shoulders started to quake and tears stung her eyes and rolled down her knees.

"This can't be happening," she muttered.

Ellen felt a warm hug around her shoulders and she looked up at Mom with tear-filled eyes. Mom had sat down beside her, and with a heavy heart she said, "What's wrong, Ellen? Did you hear the conversation I had with your dad?"

"You're going to sell Nell," Ellen blurted out.

"Ellen, we're going to do our best not to sell Nell. That would be a very last resort. Let's just hope that we get good prices for everything else. Try not to worry so much. Now, what have you done to your legs?"

Ellen swallowed and said, "I don't know. I was picking some pea vine for Nell and I'm afraid that I might have stepped into a patch of poison ivy. I know what it looks like, but I didn't see it or I wouldn't have gone there."

Mom examined Ellen's feet and ankles.

"It looks like that might be what it is all right, but we'll know for sure if blisters break out. Goodness, Ellen. You need to be more careful, especially in bare feet. In the meantime, let's go indoors and I'll get the small basin ready. You can soak your feet in it and see if that helps any. Now, dry your eyes and stop worrying. Everything will turn out all right."

The next morning, after a restless night of turning and tossing, Ellen awoke with burning blisters on the bottom of her feet. Mom sat on the edge of Ellen's bed and with a straight steel needle popped the newly formed blisters that were symptomatic of poison ivy. The needle hurt almost as much as the blisters but there was some relief when the fluid was drained from them.

Daisy watched in fascination while her mom probed the needle into the side of the blisters. There was sympathy in her voice when she asked, "Does it hurt very much?"

Ellen screwed up her face and held her ankle with both hands when Mom picked up the needle again. She said to Daisy, "It hurts like crazy. Don't ever walk into poison ivy."

William looked into the bedroom door, then came closer and took a quick look at Ellen's feet that were propped up with pillows on the end of the bed. His expression spoke both pity and understanding. He said as he started out the bedroom door, "Are you coming to school, Ellen?"

"No, I can barely walk. My feet are so sore."

"Okay then. See you later."

Ellen felt like crying again when she heard his footsteps going downstairs and the kitchen door close behind him. She wrapped the quilt around her and tried to forget the misery she was in. It was going to be a long and boring day.

Mom said that the poison ivy could last up to four weeks.

Oh, I just can't suffer through this that long, thought Ellen. She threw the quilt over her head, knocking over the books that Mom had brought up to her.

I wish I hadn't walked in poison ivy.

Ellen missed the last week of school. Her feet were just too tender to walk very far. Mom tried to keep up with the new blisters that formed while the old blisters started to heal up. Ellen kept clean socks on to cover her sore feet and gradually started to hobble around the house. She missed going to school and she missed going to the barn to see Nell even more. She could only hope that she would recover soon from the reaction to the poison ivy.

William brought home Ellen's report card and all of her notebooks and school equipment. Mom looked over Dad's shoulder while they examined it. They both started to smile with warm pride in their daughter's achievements.

"This is a great report card, Ellen. You got an A in every subject. Dad and I are so proud of you."

Dad put the report card down on the kitchen table and looked directly at William who was edging towards the hallway.

"How about yours? Didn't you get a report card as well?"

William looked down at the floor and quietly answered, "I forgot it in the barn. I can get it if you want, but I'm going back out later and I'll bring it to you then."

"I think you can go and get it right now," said Dad. "On the double."

William made a worried frown then slowly made his way back through the kitchen and out the back door. He didn't go all the way to the barn though, because his report card was laying between his books that were sitting on a log near the back door. He handed the report to his dad and started out of the kitchen, until Dad called him back and told him to stay where he was. Unfortunately, William's report didn't make as good an impression on Mom and Dad as Ellen's did when they read it. Mom just smiled knowingly and looked at Dad who gave William a stern look and said, "I guess you're more cut out for farm work than you are for school. I told you, Kate. The boy wasn't made to sit in a desk all day."

"I still passed into Grade 7," said William.

"Barely!" said Mom.

"Yes, well, let's get going outside, William. We've got work to do."

"Don't you want to see my report card?" said Daisy.

"Oh, of course I do. Let's have a look at it."

Mom and Dad enjoyed reading what Miss Larson had to say about their third child. Daisy watched them while giving William a triumphant glance.

"Good work, Daisy. Keep it up and we'll have two scholars," said Dad. Mom went back to work scalding canning jars in the big black pot on their stove. The pleasure she felt in her daughter's accomplishments was clouded by the knowledge that Ellen might not be able to continue with her studies.

I wonder if there is any way, she thought as the hot water bubbled and spit frantically around the glass jars she was sterilizing.

The day of the community picnic arrived on a beautiful sunny Sunday morning. The chores were done early and everyone was scurrying about getting ready to leave for the fun filled picnic and races. Ellen hobbled around on her blistered and painful feet, but she decided that she would go even if she had to just sit and watch the merrymaking. Restless, she thought, if I have to stay in this house one more day, I'm going to go absolutely crazy.

The aroma of Mom's baked pies filled and tantalized the kitchen. Some were still hot, bubbling with lively red fruit surrounded by golden and browned crusty pastry. They were proudly lined up on the kitchen table waiting for Mom to collect them and put them into the basket to take to the picnic. Mom's saskatoon pies were famous and would go over well with the hungry picnickers. Mom took the glass jars off the stove and threw a clean towel over them for later when she would start filling them with rhubarb jam.

Outside, Dad filled the bottom of the wagon with gunny sacks and a bag full of spoons for the egg and spoon race. Mom lined her basket with a red and white checker cloth, placed the pies inside, then closed the lid and fastened the leather strap on it. She carried the wicker basket on one arm by the strong wicker handle and the basket was carefully placed at the back of the wagon. William, after he gathered and cleaned the fresh eggs and placed them in a basket, hung on to them on his lap to avoid any cracks or breakages on the way to the picnic. They all piled into the wagon, including Ellen with her feet covered with clean socks and shoes and Tommy cuddled into Mom's lap, and with a brisk "giddap!" off they went to the field beside the community center. Even Molly got a ride to the picnic on Daisy's lap.

For a while, as they raced towards the community hall, Ellen forgot to worry about the upcoming auction and after a week of being confined with blistered feet she looked forward to socializing with her friends at the community picnic.

Chapter 16
A Picnic Prank

"I still think that moonshine should have been reported to the RCMP," said Mom.

"Kate, I told you. You need to forget about it. It's none of our business," said Dad.

"It is our business. Decent folk don't drink alcohol and I'm shocked that you would ignore such a thing."

Dad just shook his head and flicked the reins. He had no intention of making a fuss about the moonshine made in the hidden still. Nell and Sal seemed to nod their heads together in agreement as they hurried on in the broad sunshine pulling the wagon with the family in it to the picnic.

The picnic was potluck with a variety of dishes filled with savoury meats, salads and vegetables set up on tables at the picnic site. It was a blurred rainbow of colours, yellows, greens and reds and enticing scents that drifted into the air around the tables that were set up. Mom placed her pies alongside a fluffy chocolate cake at the end with the other desserts. Beside the desserts was a large swollen pot-bellied glass bowl, glistening like a sunny prism in the warm sunlight, accompanied by a number of empty cups that were stacked and ready to be used by thirsty picnickers.

Jenny Stuart was busy filling the bowl with fresh water, and from a container that she'd brought from home, she poured the juice she'd squeezed from several lemons and sugar. Small pieces of lemon pulp and the occasional lemon seed floated around the perimeter in the pale golden liquid that was contained by the glass bowl.

"Let's get lined up for the first race," called Dad after he laid out the gunny sacks at the start of the race. Jonathon Reid and Calvin Stuart were at the finish line and their friends, neighbours and families lined the racing area to shout encouragement for their favourite contestant.

Ellen sat down on the multi coloured quilt Mom put down on the grass and watched her little brother, Tommy, while he slept in the wicker basket beside her. Mom tucked a soft light blanket around his waist and into the sides of the basket before she left him in Ellen's charge. He was fast asleep, content and unaware of the noises around him.

"Aren't you going in the race?" said a voice from behind Ellen.

Ellen turned and looked up at George who was standing at the edge of the quilt and smiling at her.

"My feet are too sore, so I'm just going to watch," said Ellen.

"I heard something about that. We missed you at school this week."

George sat down beside Ellen and looked at her covered feet. Her white cotton socks were pulled up to cover her ankles. It seemed warm outside for the socks and shoes she was wearing, and George was curious about how it happened. Ellen tucked her dress around her knees and smiled at George.

"Yeah, I missed going to school. It's boring at home all day when you can't walk very far. It's different when you can move around and do stuff."

"Does it hurt much?"

"The blisters keep coming, making it hard for them to heal up."

"How did it happen?"

"I was herding our cows home from the muskeg and I decided to pick some pea vine for Nell. I was in bare feet and I must have walked into a patch of poison ivy."

"I'm in bare feet all the time," said George.

"I know. Me too, but I won't ever go barefoot again. The poison ivy is really miserable."

"How did you do with your final marks?"

"Pretty good. Mom and Dad were happy," said Ellen smiling.

George's eyes smiled back at Ellen and he said, "You're a good student. You deserved to get a good report card." Then he continued, "I passed everything. What are you going to do next year, Ellen?"

"I don't know. I want to go to Grade 9 but with everything that's going on I don't know if that's possible."

"You've got as much as you need."

"Not enough for me. I want to finish school, then travel to see more of the world."

"I just want to get married, I mean when I'm old enough, and work on the farm."

"Not me. I'm not getting married. I want to try life in the city. There are so many more things to see and do. I don't want to live on a farm when I grow up. I mean I'm happy and everything but I just can't help but feel that there's more out there. I want to experience other things. Don't you think it would be great to have a job in the city?"

"I don't know what I would do in a city. All I know is farming and there really isn't very much money to go anywhere."

Ellen added wistfully, "You're right. There isn't much money."

"Come on, George. We need you for the three legged race," called William.

"Gotta go," said George. "Talk to you later."

Ellen stayed on the quilt with Tommy and as she shifted she caught sight of the pimple faced lad that had asked her to dance a while ago at the community dance. In the sunlight he looked older than she remembered and somehow a little bit rougher. He was wearing the same red plaid shirt but it was only partly tucked in to his pants and his hair was disheveled, making him look like he'd been up all night. He was standing near the lemonade bowl at the end of the picnic table and when the line up for a drink disappeared, glanced around to see if anyone was watching him while he pulled a silver flask from his pocket and poured a liquid from it into the lemonade. There was only about a third of the lemonade left because most people had already had a drink. Racing was thirsty work.

What's he doing thought Ellen. He shouldn't be doing that. Her eyes widened as a realization washed over her. I bet he's got some of that moonshine Mom was talking about. I bet he's the one that's making the alcohol in the still that's hidden in the bog.

He looked up from his sneaky job and saw Ellen staring at him, gave her a sly grin and winked at her.

Ellen's cheeks coloured and she immediately looked down and adjusted Tommy's blanket around him. When Ellen looked up again the pimple faced lad was gone.

Mom appeared at the picnic table and scooped a ladle full of the lemonade into her glass, and before Ellen could get up off of the quilt and talk to her, she quickly drank it all in one gulp.

Oh, oh, thought Ellen, but she stayed on the quilt and decided to just watch and see what happened. Tommy stirred in his basket and Ellen looked down at her awakening baby brother. She was about to pick him up but his fluttering eyes closed again. He gave a quivering sigh then his breathing relaxed back into contented sleep. While Ellen was busy checking Tommy, Mom turned around and found her way back to the end of the picnic table again where the lemonade was sitting.

"Boy, am I ever thirsty and this is so good," she said with a happy grin, and she promptly drank another glass of lemonade.

Ellen's head jerked up when she heard her mom say in a very loud voice, "Come on, Billy. Get your legs in gear and win that race!"

Mom teetered back towards the races and laughing said, "Billy boy! Come on, move your ass!"

Did she just say 'ass' thought Ellen. Oh dear. I'd better talk to Dad right away. What did he put in that lemonade anyway? Oh, dear.

At the start of the race that went around the field two times, Dad was in the starting position, his face intent. Dad was slender and could run like the wind. He had an abundance of physical stamina and had won many first prizes for his sprints at the local picnics and sports events. He looked back from the starting line at his giggling wife and frowned, then refocused on starting his race.

Mom walked up to Sara Saunders who was standing with a group of ladies watching the races from one side and gave her a hearty slap on her back. The slap nearly knocked her off her feet but she recovered from the forward jerk.

"Hi there, neighbor! How are things in your neck of the woods?" slurred a loud and chuckling Mom.

"Have you tried the lemonade? You should try it. It sure is good."

Sara Saunders looked at Mom's rosy face in astonishment but didn't answer her. Sara and Jenny Stuart were standing with Becky Reid and Lucy MacDonald, and the shock slowly spread over their incredulous faces as the group of women looked at each other in stunned silence. Their eyes followed Mom, mouths agape.

"What's the matter? Don't feel sociable?" said Mom a little too loudly, and she tripped back to the table with the lemonade on it.

"Whoever made this lemonade should be complemented. It's greeeeat!" said Mom, as she gulped down another glass.

The other women watched Mom, then huddled and whispered to each other.

"I do think Kate Graham is inebriated," said Sara Saunders to Jenny Stuart.

"Well, I knew they had some problems, but really."

"I don't know. There's something funny here. She's been drinking the lemonade. What did you put in it?" said Sara to Jenny.

"Why I didn't put anything extra in it, just water, sugar and some juice from squeezed lemons."

"Are you sure? I don't recall ever getting that reaction just from lemonade."

"Of course I'm sure. I wonder if someone spiked the lemonade."

"Oh, my goodness," they all said to each other and the women moved closer to each other trying to hide their laughter.

Mom gave out a loud hiccup followed by some more giggles as she walked back towards the races.

Ellen nervously looked around until she spotted Daisy sitting on the grass holding Molly under her arm and talking to her friend, Helen. In the heat of the clear afternoon air, the sun bounced off of their shiny hair and animated faces. While keeping one eye on the basket, she asked Daisy to come and help watch Tommy while she went to find Dad.

"Why do I have to watch Tommy? Isn't it your job?"

"Because I need to talk to Dad and I don't want to carry Tommy's basket."

Daisy's mouth curled up in a pout until Ellen said, "Daisy, there's lots of room on the quilt for both you and Helen. Just stay here until I get back. The quilt is nicer to sit on than the grass anyway."

Daisy agreed, and carrying Molly, both of the girls sat down beside Tommy's basket on the quilt. Ellen glanced at the lemonade bowl but Mom wasn't there. In fact Mom was nowhere to be seen.

As Ellen approached the races she heard the roar from the crowd and the murmurs of congratulations that accompanied the end of the sprint that Dad was in. He was surrounded by his neighbours who were patting him on the back and talking all at the same time.

"Good race, Billy! You did it again."

"You were way out in front again. Way to go!"

"Dad! Dad I need to talk to you," said Ellen.

Dad looked up at Ellen. He was still breathing fast and there were beads of sweat on his forehead.

He wiped his shiny face with his arm and finally said between pants,

"What's wrong, Ellen? Is something wrong with Tommy?"

"No, Dad. I just need to talk to you. Over here," Ellen gestured and Dad followed.

"Dad, something is wrong with Mom," she said.

"What do you mean? Is she sick?"

"I saw a guy over there, the one that was at the dance last month. Anyway, I saw him put something into the lemonade, and Mom has had three drinks of it. She's acting silly and giggly."

Dad closed his eyes, paused, then said,

"Four."

"Four?" said Ellen.

"I think she's had four drinks. I brought her a glassful just before I lined up to race. Do you know what it was that he put in it?"

"No, but it was in the silver flask that he had alcohol in at the dance."

Dad saw Mom tripping unsteadily towards him. She was chuckling to herself and what was more she was singing too. He looked down trying to stifle his chuckles. Finally, he said, "Ellen, she might have a headache in the morning but your mom will be all right. I think she accidentally drank some moonshine."

"Moonshine," repeated Ellen. "That's what I was afraid of. What are you going to do?"

"Not much I can do. We'll try to get her home as soon as possible."

"Are you sure she'll be all right?"

"Don't worry. I'll take care of it."

"But, Dad. We can't go home now. We haven't eaten yet."

"The races are done. You kids can eat quickly and I'll try and keep Mom quiet. There might be some coffee made. That might help."

Dad put his arm around Mom's shoulder, and smiling, Mom wrapped her arm around Dad's waist and with her head tilted towards his shoulder she followed him to a grassy spot under a tree away from their neighbours.

Ellen sat down beside Mom under the tree and let her put her head on her shoulder. Mom's face was flushed and she gave a happy sigh before saying,

"I'm dizzy. The whole world is turning around and around."

"Just sit here and stay still. Don't move and don't drink any more lemonade. I'll be right back."

Dad raced back to the picnic table where the lemonade bowl sat. He sniffed it but there was no telltale odour. Then he tasted the lemonade. There was a faint zing to it and he paused for another chuckle. Kate was drunk.

"What's the problem?" said Jonathan Reid.

"It seems that someone put moonshine into the lemonade and Kate drank some. She's not feeling too good."

"Good grief. Who would do that?"

"I don't know who it was. Ellen saw him pouring it from a silver flask."

"Here, let's get rid of what's left of the lemonade and hopefully no one else drank any of it."

Dad poured it out on the ground, the pallid drink rippled then gathered into a puddle and disappeared into the glistening grass leaving behind some fragments of lemon pulp. Then he looked around for the culprit but he was nowhere to be seen.

When William went by, Dad motioned to him to come to the quilt where Daisy and Tommy were. Dad looked at William's face a little closer. He could see greasy crumbs from the fried chicken on the corners of his mouth.

"What?" said William.

"Have you been into the fried chicken?"

"No, well, maybe… Yes. But I was hungry."

"You're always hungry. Can't you wait like everyone else?"

William just looked down. His dad wasn't aware of the chocolate cookies that he'd stuffed into his back pockets. William could feel them starting to crumble when he sat down on them but he didn't dare try to take them out until Dad left.

"We're going to have to eat soon and head for home."

"Why? We're just starting to have fun."

"Mom's not feeling well."

"She looks fine to me."

"No arguments. Just do as you're told."

William looked anxiously over at the picnic table and remembered all the food he'd inspected. His mouth watered at the thought of all the feasting that was about to start.

Dad picked up Tommy's basket and took him back to the tree where Mom was resting. Mom's eyes were closed but she was smiling and singing to herself,

"shine on, shine on harvest moon."

Dad put Tommy down beside Ellen and said, "I'm going to get some plates of food for you and your Mom. She'll feel better when she's had something to eat. I couldn't find any coffee."

"for me and my gal," sang Mom.

The Graham family quickly had something to eat, and then Dad loaded up the wagon with the pie plates in the basket, the sacks and the spoons. Then he quickly got the children into the wagon before he helped Mom up from the grass.

"Bye everyone! Great picnic," called Mom very loudly, waving as she staggered into the wagon with Dad's help. Her happy head rested on Dad's shoulder while she sang to herself. Dad just snickered and flicked the reins urging Nell and Sal home. Mom continued her serenade and giggles all the way home. Her children were silent, even Tommy.

Once they were home, Dad with Mom's arm wrapped around his neck climbed the stairs that led to their bedroom and into their bed.

"I'm tired," mumbled Mom.

"You'll be all right once you've had some sleep," said Dad.

"Good picnic, wasn't it? I haven't had that much fun in a long time."

"Yes, Kate. It was a good picnic. Now off to bed."

Dad helped her get undressed and slipped her white cotton nightgown over her head. The flowers that were printed on the wallboard were animated and smiling at her in the long summer evening light. Mom's limbs felt like jelly when she flopped down on the bed and closed her eyes, drifting into sleepy oblivion.

Tommy was awake now and hungry too, so Dad put some warmed cow's milk into a bottle for him and Ellen sat down in the rocking chair in the parlour. She held him with his little head nestled into her arm and she fed him the milk from the bottle. At first Tommy spit the nipple of the bottle out but after a few tries he was content with the milk Dad had warmed for him.

With his head down, Dad walked back down the path to the barn to feed and water the animals. He stopped just before he entered, looked up and stared silently at the new poster that had been nailed to the outside of his barn door. His chuckles evaporated into the worry lines that deepened in his face when he read what it said.

Tax Lien Auction
A public auction will be held
At 10:00 a.m.
On the last Monday in September.

Chapter 17
Cream Rustling

"Hey there, Nell," said Ellen as she set down the grain pail she was carrying. "Brought you some treats."

Nell swung her head over the stall door and whinnied softly in greeting. Curious, she nuzzled Ellen's outstretched hand, nudged around her body tickling her then sniffed her pockets in search of the promised snacks.

"Here they are," she said to Nell.

Ellen could feel Nell's warm breath gusting on her hand when she slid two carrots from the back pockets of her overalls, and with a couple of swipes on the front leg of her pants she cleaned some of the gritty sandy soil that clung to the crevices in the carrots. Nell wrapped her lips around one carrot and with her teeth gave it a good pull into her mouth. Nell showed her appreciation with noisy munching and in large circular motions crunched the carrot into pieces, finishing off with the green leafy top. Like an acrobat at the circus, Ellen's mind tumbled and pitched, always returning to the upcoming farm auction.

Oh, God. Please make the auction go well so Mom and Dad won't have to sell Nell, Ellen silently prayed.

The auction was being held bright and early next Saturday morning at their farm and Ellen grew more worried as that day drew nearer. Time was running out.

"I hope you never leave us," Ellen whispered while she gave Nell a hug around her neck.

I wonder what Daisy is up to, she thought as she plodded back to the house.

Mom, Tommy and Dad left early to go to Pratt and she was left in charge of the chores and Daisy. Ellen felt the weight of the world on her as she thought, I can't remember why Mom and Dad went to Pratt. I could have gone if it was just for the mail. It would have been a good excuse to ride Nell. Ellen looked at the open road and thought, maybe we could have just kept on going. Oh well, that's silly. I wouldn't know where to go. Mom says that they probably won't have to sell Nell but I don't believe her. I think they'll have to sell everything in order to come up with the money to pay the taxes. I wonder where William went. Probably fishing or something. Why couldn't he stay home and help once in a while? Must be nice to be a boy."

The screen door squealed as she swung it towards her and bounced it wide open. Ellen thumped into the kitchen and her pensiveness was suddenly shaken off by the scene in front of her.

"Daisy! What have you been doing?" said Ellen.

Daisy looked around at Ellen from her perch on a wooden stool she was standing on. She was wearing Mom's apron over her dress and was stirring a yellow ceramic bowl full of gooey white dough. The apron reached down past Daisy's feet to the floor, and the top of it bloused out where it was gathered to fit around Daisy's small waist.

"Uh, I'm making dumplings."

"Dumplings? Daisy, you don't know how to make dumplings."

"Yes, I do. The recipe is right here. I can read. I want to surprise Mom by making dinner."

"Oh, she'll be surprised all right. What a mess you've made."

"Tis not a mess. And anyways I'll clean it up."

"What did you mix up anyway?"

"Flour, salt, baking powder and water."

"Then what will you do with it?"

"I don't know. It just tells me what to mix up. I don't know how to cook it."

Daisy lifted up a large wooden serving spoonful of the lumpy anemic dough. It was heavy and fell off the spoon and into the bowl with a thud.

"I followed the recipe," said Daisy, her lower lip quivering.

Ellen groaned as she looked around at the flour spattered counter and table top and the sticky fingerprints on the cupboard doors. Even her feet stuck to the floor when she took a few steps forward. The wooden table that had been cleaned and polished after breakfast was now littered with Mom's measuring spoons, cups, two large metal pots, and lumps of wet dough stuck to Mom's ceramic bowls that were heavily coated with the pasty goo crusting around their rims. In the middle of this was Mom's spattered cookbook, opened to the page headed, "Dumplings."

Mom's measuring tablespoon was stuck to the open page of the cookbook threatening to become a permanent section of the recipe. The metal water dipper lay dripping on the counter beside a small sack of flour. Even Molly, sitting on Dad's wooden chair had bits of dough stuck to the top of her yellow woolen hair and her permanently smiling face.

"Daisy, you can't make dumplings unless you have soup or stew to cook them in."

"I didn't know that."

"We'd better start cleaning this mess up before Mom and Dad get home. They should be here any minute."

"I'm sorry, Ellen."

"Never mind being sorry. Just get down from there and let's start getting the dishes washed and things put away."

"I just wanted to make Mom happy," said Daisy.

"Okay, well, she'll be a lot happier if she doesn't see this mess."

"What mess?" said a voice coming towards the kitchen from the hallway.

"I was just trying to help," pleaded Daisy.

Mom surveyed the now confused kitchen. Her mouth opened as if to say something then looking down she silently shook her head. When she regained her composure she was able to say,

"What are you doing?"

"I'm making dumplings."

"Dumplings!"

"All right, Daisy. You need to clean up the mess now."

"Can't I make the dumplings?"

"Not today, I'm afraid. Maybe someday soon I'll teach you the correct way to make dumplings. Ellen, get some hot water heated and we'll start washing these dishes before the dough dries hard on them."

"I'll leave this letter in the parlour until you have time to look at it," said Dad and he made his way through the topsy turvy kitchen and down the hallway. Mom untied her apron from around Daisy's waist and slipped into it, tying it around herself with a firm knot at the back and avoiding the wet gooey dough that graced the front of it. Dad's announcement was lost in the busy clatter of cleaning up Daisy's kitchen caper.

When they all sat down to eat, their normal happy dinner chatter evaporated into the silent air. William and Ellen were lost in their own thoughts and Daisy just looked at Ellen, then William, Mom and Dad.

Finally, Mom broke the silence, "You know, I'm certain how many jars of cream I put down the well. There were three jars yesterday and three jars the day before. I would swear to that. Out of all of that there were only two jars of cream when I looked this morning. I have three more jars to put down there but I'm afraid something or someone is stealing our cream. Last week some cream was missing too. I'm sure of it. I don't think I should put the cream out there this evening."

After a thoughtful pause, Dad said,

"Yeah, you know. I think you should put the cream down in the well. Same as usual."

"But, Billy. What if it's gone in the morning?"

"Just put it down there. We'll see what happens tonight. In fact, I'll take it out myself, and William, I think after dinner that you and I should have a good look around the well. You never know what might be going on."

Dinner was finished and the dishes washed and put away. The newly scrubbed kitchen was not looking any worse for the disarray of Daisy's cooking. It was shining and clean, ready to greet the family for their next meal.

Later that evening, Mom sat down in the rocking chair in the parlour with Tommy. He was hungry again and it was a peaceful time away from the stormy thoughts in her mind. Mom glanced at the letter that Dad had placed on the end table and she thought, I almost forgot. I'll have a look at that when Tommy goes to sleep. Right now I'm just too tired to think of anything.

A curtain of darkness descended and the warm summer sun said its brilliant farewell to the day with a summons for the family to rest.

"Daisy, are you in bed?" said Mom.

Daisy didn't answer but Ellen poked her head into the doorway of the parlour and said,

"She's already in bed sleeping and I'm on my way up. I think William might have gone to bed too but I'm not sure."

"All right, Ellen. I'll see you in the morning."

Carrying a book under her arm, Ellen climbed the stairs to her and Daisy's bedroom. After reading the same page for fifteen minutes, Ellen gave up and turned down the humming lamp. She drifted off to sleep curled up next to her sister in their cozy bed.

Downstairs, in the parlour, Mom's eyes grew heavy and her breathing flowed longer and deeper. She was sleeping upright with her head nodding but still with a firm grip on her child. Tommy was still nursing sporadically between long breaths and fluttering eyelids. Finally he gave way and with a sigh slipped into dreamy serene slumbering. It seemed that the whole farmhouse drifted into quiet and peaceful repose.

They had been sleeping for about an hour when a loud bang that shook the nails in the walls and rattled the windows awakened everyone from their sleep. Mom started in her surprise. For a moment she couldn't remember where she was in the darkened parlour, confused for a moment until the blind foggy dozing was replaced by clear consciousness. Tommy stirred in her arms just as another bang boomed like a thunderbolt, jarring the air and shaking Mom. She nearly knocked over the side table that was beside her. With her free hand, she felt for the coal oil lamp and turned it up so that she could see better. Mom didn't notice that in the confusion she had knocked the letter off the side table onto the floor and under the sofa.

"Mom, what was that terrible noise?" said Ellen from the top of the staircase. Daisy was peeking around from behind her.

"William's not in his room," said Ellen. "Is someone shooting? That sounded like a gun going off."

"It sure did. I don't know where your dad is either," said Mom and carrying Tommy she entered the dark hallway.

"Don't go outside, Mom. Not until we know what's going on."

Mom hesitated. She was sure she could hear male voices shouting. The girls followed their mom down the hallway and into the kitchen.

"Oh, no. Please don't go out there, Mom," wailed Daisy.

Another bang rang out further away from the house and, after the noise, yelling voices were heard retreating away from the farmhouse.

Frozen, they huddled near the kitchen door, waiting for the next report, but not wanting to go outside to see what was happening.

The kitchen door suddenly swung open with a force that made them jump. Ellen held her breath and stared at Dad and William standing in the doorway. Dad was carrying his shotgun in one hand

and a lantern in the other. He was dressed in dark clothes with a dark hat pulled down to the top of his vengeful eyes. A quiet snicker graced his face when he and William entered the kitchen.

"I got him!" Dad said.

"We sure did," said William.

"Got who? Who did you get?" questioned Mom as she put Tommy down on the bed in the spare bedroom off of the kitchen.

"Billy, you didn't shoot anyone, did you?"

"You bet we did," chuckled William.

"We got that blood sucking thief," said Dad. "He won't be back, not for a long time. It'll take some time to dig the buckshot out of his butt."

"Was he the one that was stealing our cream?"

"Sure was. He didn't get any tonight though. We waited, hiding in the dark, just beside the barn and sure enough he showed up, that dirty weasel of a thief."

"How did you see him?"

"I set up a wire over the top of the well. It had a bell on it so we waited and when the bell started to ring I knew someone was there."

"Who was it? Did you get a look at him?"

"It was hard to tell in the dark so I can't be sure.

He's got a fat belly and a crooked walk that slowed him down a bit when he was running away. Other than that I didn't see his face but he had long hair sticking out of his hat. He'll have a sore rear though. We'll just watch for someone that can't sit down for very long."

"Was he riding a horse?"

"I think his horse was waiting for him down the road a ways."

Mom sat down on a kitchen chair and leaned her head on one hand. Once she recovered from the evening's startling event she relaxed into a soft giggle that rose to a crescendo of laughter. The amusement spread throughout the kitchen until tears stung their eyes and their cheeks grew rosy with their own heat.

Tommy joined in with a cry for Mom who promptly got up and went to pick him up. Eventually the whole family was settled back down into restful sleep and the cream that was in the well was left safely intact.

Chapter 18
Mom's Letter

The next evening, after the supper dishes were put into hot soapy water to be washed, Dad stopped on his way outside and said,

"Did you ever read that letter, Kate?'

"What letter?"

"The one we picked up in Pratt. I put it on the end table in the parlour for you to read."

"Oh, I forgot all about it. That's right. It was there last night. I saw it when I sat down to feed Tommy but haven't seen it since. After last night's shooting adventure I couldn't find it. Are you sure you didn't move it?"

"No, I haven't even been in there. I've been so busy getting ready for the auction."

"Ellen, William, have you seen the letter that was sitting on the end table in the parlour? Did anyone move it?"

They both shook their heads and said that they hadn't seen it anywhere. Mom decided that she'd better have a look for it. She went into the parlour and quickly looked around the area but the letter was nowhere obvious.

It must be hiding somewhere she thought.

Mom started a more careful search. She picked up the cushions on the sofa to see if it had somehow slipped between the cushion and its back, then felt along the back and down the arms of the sofa but no letter was found. She took the white crocheted doily off of the end table, noting the layer of dust underneath the doily, but still no letter could be seen. She inspected the floor, lifting the oval braided rug but again the elusive letter was nowhere to be found. Ellen, William and Daisy followed their Mom's movements from the doorway but they didn't see any sign of the letter either.

"Oh, well. I guess it'll turn up someday. I wonder what happened to it? It was here only last night. I've got to get some work done while Tommy is sleeping. I'll take another look a bit later," said Mom, retreating back into her busy kitchen.

The week was going by very quickly. Dad hoped that they would get a good crowd gathered at his auction on Saturday morning. He told as many people as he could about it and made sure that announcements were posted in Pratt and Holland.

Ellen spent most of her time hidden away in the barn, her thoughts alternating between taking Nell away with her and telling people that buying Nell wasn't a good idea because Nell was a little bit crazy and only she knew how to handle her. William spent his time helping Dad get things cleaned up and ready for public inspection.

Daisy, feeling a little ignored, was playing with Molly in the parlour.

"Let's go to town today, Molly. We can ride in the wagon and maybe have tea with my friend, Helen. There you go. You need to change your clothes."

Molly was in a state of undress, her soft puffy cotton body was only covered by the checker bloomers that were gathered with elastic around her waist and upper legs. Her silent smiling face looked into the distance, waiting and unresponsive. Daisy found her little dress that had been left in her cradle and slipped it over her floppy head, then closed the metal snaps at the back. Then she started to look for Molly's red woolen sweater.

I know it's here somewhere she thought and got down on her hands and knees to get a better look on the floor. She caught sight of a patch of red just sitting under the sofa near the outside corner.

There it is. It's under the sofa.

Daisy pulled the tiny sweater out. She was surprised to see that underneath it was a white envelope. It was sealed with a letter inside of it.

"Mom, is this the letter you've been looking for?"

Daisy was answered with silence.

Mom must be busy with Tommy she sighed. I'll just put it in the kitchen where she'll see it. Daisy stood up and walked into the kitchen.

"Mom, are you in here?"

Daisy looked in the spare bedroom where she was sometimes feeding Tommy. Mom was nowhere to be seen.

I'll just leave it here on the counter where she'll find it thought Daisy, and she went back into the parlour and finished dressing Molly for their pretend outing.

William had been out in the chicken house gathering eggs and he entered through the back door carrying his wire basket full of fresh ones. He was in a hurry so he quickly plopped the basket down on the counter and headed back outside barely looking at where the basket was placed. The unfortunate letter lay directly under the basket carrying William's eggs.

Later in the day when Mom, with Ellen's help, was busy preparing their dinner. Daisy came through the door and said,

"I found it, Mom. I found your letter."

"Where was it?"

"It was underneath Molly's jacket under the sofa. I found it when I was playing with Molly."

"Where is it now?"

"I put it on the counter."

"On the counter? I don't see it now. Are you sure that's where you put it?"

After a thoughtful moment Daisy said that she had put it beside the blue crock pot on the counter.

"It couldn't have gone very far," said Mom glancing up and down the counter.

Mom with Ellen's help looked everywhere in the kitchen. They thought that perhaps it had fallen on the floor again but there was no sign of the letter anywhere. They looked the counter over, not once, but several times but they couldn't see the lost letter. They even picked up the egg basket but they didn't see anything underneath it. They checked the table and even inside the cupboards but no letter was found.

"That letter just doesn't want to get read. It can't have vanished into thin air again," said Mom. "It's probably nothing important anyway," she mumbled to herself. "I've got so much to do I really don't have time to search for letters."

After dinner, Ellen was busy washing the dishes, and her reddened hands were hot in the soapy water. She was trying to hurry so she could go out to the barn.

The dishes were all clean and dried when she noticed the basket sitting there with the eggs in it. She hurriedly picked up the basket and started to dunk the eggs, basket and all into the warm water in the sink. The letter that was covered by the basket was stuck to the bottom of the wire basket and nearly went for a swim in the dishwater before Ellen noticed the white corners just as they were going in. She was able to retrieve the envelope containing the letter before it was completely soaked and laid it out on the table, then called Mom to come and look at it.

Mom came into the kitchen and picked up the dodging letter. The envelope threatened to dissolve in her hands and the addresses were a blur of blue ink but when she opened it the letter inside was still readable. Weary, Mom sat down on a chair at the kitchen table. The tiredness in her legs ached in relief and her eyes that focused a questioning frown before the letter's contents started to make sense to her.

"What does it say, Mom?" asked Ellen.

"I don't really understand what these people want," replied Mom. "Ellen, I think your dad is close by. Will you go and get him? I'd like to talk to him about it."

Without saying anything more, Ellen headed out the back door to find Dad. When they returned, Dad asked,

"What's all this about?"

"I don't know. I thought perhaps you could make some sense out of it,"

"Let's have a look at it."

Ellen, William and Daisy watched their parents, curious to know what was inside the letter that had been missing for a few days. Mom sat down at the table and unfolded the letter again. Its dampened corners didn't compromise the message that was written inside. It said:

> Dear Mrs. Graham,
>
> It is of the utmost importance that you meet with me at my office in Holland. I hope to see you at your earliest available convenience.
>
> Sincerely,
>
> Edward J. Harvard
> Notary Public

Mom and Dad looked at each other, then back at the letter.

"I don't trust it," said Dad.

"We don't know what he wants," said Mom.

"We can't go this week, Kate. There's just too much work to do."

Dad abruptly got up from his chair and went outside without saying another word. Mom sat in the chair a little longer, puzzling about what this notary public could possibly want from them.

Is it something to do with our farm and the taxes she thought. Her gaze into the air was distant and clouded by worry until she was brought back to life when Tommy started to fuss.

I'd better get the little guy fed and changed, then I'll think about it she thought.

As the day's light faded into darkness Dad, weary from his long day of working, came into the house. He was silent, lost in his own thoughts throughout their evening meal and then he silently went back outside to finish the jobs that were unfinished. Mom was sitting in the rocking chair with Tommy staring off into space, wondering what the letter meant and what this notary public person wanted to speak to them about. Dad quietly sat down beside her and tiredly said, "I guess we should go and deal with this problem as soon as we can. I have everything caught up with and we can go first thing in the morning."

Mom nodded a weary agreement and Dad continued, "I don't like it. I'm going to tell that man, whatever his name is, that we're doing our best to pay our taxes. They've got to understand that we should be able to pay them after Saturday."

"One thing I don't understand," said Mom. "Why was the letter addressed to me and not to both of us?"

"I don't understand either. Maybe it was a mistake but I guess we'll find out tomorrow. We'd better get to bed so we can get a good start tomorrow morning. It'll be good to get it over with. Otherwise we'll be worrying about it all weekend."

"Yes, I guess that's what we need to do. I'll be up in a moment and we'll all try and get some sleep," said Mom.

Mom heard the creaking stairs as Dad mounted them up to their bedroom. Guided by the crowning yellow glow in their bedroom, she turned the light out and carrying Tommy, she followed Dad up the stairs.

They left very early in the morning after waking Ellen and telling her where they were going and leaving instructions for her. Tommy went with them, comfortable on Mom's lap as Dad flicked the reins hurrying Nell and Sal along. He was anxious to get this errand over with and return home again as quickly as possible.

"Oh, Billy. Just look at the sunrise. It's going to be a beautiful day!"

Dad looked up at the pale blue that blended into pale yellow, then orange and pink on the horizon, greeting the glowing gold sun as its glittering beams radiated from behind the distant hills. It said to them that the world was still a glorious place, even in the midst of struggles and challenges. They rode in silence, bathed in a glow of peaceful delight.

Once they arrived in Holland, Dad stopped on the main road and they both looked at the envelope and the letter.

"I don't know where the notary public's office is," said Dad.

"I've been trying to read the return address on the envelope but I'm afraid the blue ink is too smudged to read it properly," said Mom.

"Let me have a look at it."

Dad squinted at it but he couldn't discern the name of the street or the number of the office.

"We'll just have to ask someone," said Dad, and he climbed down from the wagon and went into a little bakery that was open. He was carrying the letter and Mom could see him talking to the store clerk.

The clerk came out of the front door with Dad and pointed down the road and then pointed to the right. They both nodded their heads and Mom heard Dad say, "Thanks, I should be able to find it now."

Dad returned to the wagon with the wonderful aroma of fresh bread and sweet confections following him.

They found the notary public office nestled amongst a row of small green and white buildings that were joined together at the end of Fourth Street. The office was shared with an insurance agent's office. Dad grimaced when he noted the all too familiar RCMP office just across the street, the provincial government land office two doors down, and the National bank on the same side of the street as the notary public office.

Carrying Tommy and the letter, Mom climbed down from the wagon and Dad held the door to the office open for her as they went in. The young receptionist looked up from her desk and smiled,

"Yes, what can I do for you?"

"We're here to see Mr. Harvard," replied Dad.

"Do you have an appointment?" she said.

"No, but we have a letter here that says that Mr. Harvard wanted to speak with us as soon as possible."

The young woman at the desk took the letter from Mom and examined it, then got up and went through the door leading to the back office. Mom and Dad looked at each other, then down at the floor while they waited.

A tall, mustached man dressed in a smart tweed suit came briskly through the back office door to greet Mom and Dad.

"Mrs. Graham? Mrs. Katherine Graham?" he said looking at Mom.

"Yes, that's me," Mom replied. She was puzzled at his interest in her.

"I just need you to sign some papers," he said with a smile.

"What papers?" Dad inquired suspiciously.

"Didn't anyone inform you about your Aunt Dorothy?"

"What about Aunt Dorothy?" Mom and Dad said simultaneously.

"Why, she died, of course," said Mr. Harvard. "Oh, I see. You didn't know about it. I would have thought that Lydia would have written to you and explained what happened. Well, come in and sit down and I'll explain everything."

Dad followed Mom into the back office where Mr. Harvard directed them to sit down in the chairs that were placed on the other side of his desk.

"Mrs. Graham, it seems that your aunt has died and left a small inheritance to you."

Mom and Dad looked at each other, their eyes widening in disbelief. "An inheritance," they both mouthed silently.

"Inheritance! What do you mean? I knew Aunt Dorothy was sick, but I didn't realize how serious it was."

"Can you tell me what exactly my wife has inherited?" said Dad, finally grasping what they were hearing.

"Mrs. Graham has inherited the sum of $2000. Now if you could just sign here, then I can release the cheque in that amount to you."

Mom and Dad couldn't move for a few moments. They were stunned by the news that their financial difficulties were resolved. When Mom finally accepted that it was indeed true, she handed Tommy to Dad, picked up the pen and dipped the end into the bottle of black ink that sat on the side of the wide oak desk. Mom's hand felt foreign and shaky as she carefully signed her full name on the dotted line at the bottom of the document. She slowly looked up and into the dark twinkling eyes and smiling face of Mr. Harvard. In his hand he was holding the thick crisp cheque out to her. Mom took the end of it and brought it closer and examined it. It was made out in black ink to Mrs. Katherine Graham for the amount of $2000. She just couldn't believe it and sat back in her seat and stared at it for a few moments.

"Mrs. Graham, the bank is just a few doors down if you want to deposit the money into your account."

"Deposit the money," Mom repeated, mumbling, then she looked at Dad and smiled.

"Can we cash the cheque?"

"Mrs. Graham, the money is yours. You can do whatever you please with it," answered Mr. Harvard.

Looking at Dad, Mom said, "Do we have time?"

Dad was stirred out of his stunned silence.

"If we go now, we should be able to cash the cheque."

"And pay the taxes?" said Mom, with a light in her eyes.

Dad nodded, remembering that the government land office was just across the street.

"We should go and take care of that. Thank you, Mr. Harvard. Thank you very much."

Dad was smiling now as he shook hands with Mr. Harvard and he and Mom stepped out of his office and walked to the National Bank. They deposited the money into an account there and withdrew enough to pay the taxes.

"I don't have the forms with me," said Mom.

"They'll look it up for us," said Dad.

"Are you sure you know how much it is? Do we have enough?"

"Don't worry. I know exactly how much it is."

The trip home was euphoric. The symphony of colours in the rolling hills and endless blue sky were clearer and brighter than they remembered. Even

Nell and Sal moved with energy and jubilation. As they pranced towards home, Mom and Dad thought with joy that their farm was safe, their home was safe, the animals would stay in their home, and Nell wouldn't have to be sold to a stranger. They felt like singing they were so happy. Tommy felt their exuberance and he smiled and made a soft little laugh while he kicked his tiny feet in his blanket. Mom and Dad couldn't wait to tell Ellen, William and Daisy that the auction would be cancelled and that all was well at the Graham farm.

As they were riding over the last rolling hill towards their home, their farmhouse appeared. Their family waiting for them, the house, the barns, the fields with the cattle and horses in them never looked so good to them.

Chapter 19
Nell

It was that time of life when, like the road that seemed to travel forever across the landscape, her future felt like an endless journey ahead of her with nothing but time and adventures to experience. She was sixteen, filled with hope, determination and confidence in that inner voice that told her she could do just about anything.

Ellen shivered in the cool pink and grey dawn and pulled her warm hat further down her head to protect herself from the spring drizzle that hung in the air and drifted through her clothing right through to her flesh and bones. It was early June, and after a spell of warm weather in May, the uncharacteristic warmth was relieved by some cooler spring showers.

She pulled up to the last house on the milk route and turned to look at the two remaining bottles that teetered in the wooden box at the back of the milk wagon. The cool mist settled on the outside of the glass bottles, droplets of glassy moisture that trickled down the outside of them. A crown of thick golden cream that topped the lily white milk seemed to push up the small round cardboard lids that sealed the milk at the top of the thick glass necks of the bottles.

Ellen jumped out of the delivery wagon and picked up the two cold wet bottles of milk with her gloved hands. She had to be careful because they were slippery and she didn't want to drop them on the ground on her way to the front doorstep of the house.

Heaving a sigh, she walked up the stone pathway to the front door. She glanced up at the gold coloured metal doorknob that was silent on the locked white door and she put the two full bottles of milk on one side of the porch and picked up the two empty ones that the family had left there. The tattered screen door had been left unhooked and looked as though it had swung wide open and frozen there.

It must be nice to sleep in thought Ellen. What time do you get up?

The door answered with silence and Ellen turned and walked towards the milk wagon. The dozing street that stretched in front of her was lined with sleeping houses in the misty grey morning light, not yet aroused from their night time slumbering.

Ellen had been delivering milk to customers all through fall and winter and many of the mornings were pitch dark as well as being a frigid minus 40 degrees. She stayed with a family that had a dairy farm situated on the edge of town. To pay for her room and board while she went to school, her job was to deliver the milk early in the morning after the cows were milked and the milk was bottled.

As she was driving back to the farm she was overtaken with a sense of foreboding, a strange kind of loss. Was this homesickness? Perhaps she was just tired and needed some rest from the grueling routine of work and school. Still, it was hard to shake this unsettled feeling. That heavy grey damp sensation followed her all the way back to the Schulz' dairy farm. Mr. and Mrs. Schulz tried very hard to make her feel at home but she missed her family. Even when Mrs. Schulz made those wonderful German pastries and tarts and the aroma of fresh baking filled the air, Ellen felt that it just couldn't compare with Mom's saskatoon pies and homemade bread.

On her way up to her tiny room at the top of the stairs, she carried a mug of hot tea with milk and sugar in it, then settled in with a warm quilt wrapped around her legs and relaxed into an over-stuffed chair that sat in one corner of her semi-darkened room. Her memories chased each other in her mind, seeming to rise then evaporate like the steam from her piping hot tea. The soothing heat of the hot mug felt good in her cold hands that were wrapped around the mug, and she sighed as she breathed in the calming warmth.

It was Sunday morning and she couldn't quite shake the habit Mom had ingrained in the family that Sunday was a day of rest and so she spent what was left of her morning remembering her life with her family on the farm.

She thought about the red brick house, her home, where she'd grown up, and the family dinners with the happy chatter that surrounded them as they ate. It was quiet and strained at the Schulz table with only Mr. Schulz's occasional grunts and queries about how long it took her to deliver the milk to all of their customers.

"Dats gut," he would say between mouthfuls.

She thought about William teasing her on their rides to school and back, and wondered what George was doing. William said that he was helping his dad on their farm. There was always so much work to do. William was growing tall and was developing a young man's strong shoulders and arms. He looked so handsome the last time she'd seen him.

The young people in her class at school were nice, but she missed her friends from the little Rae school at home. She smiled as she recalled the fun she'd had playing her guitar with her dad at the community dances, and she remembered the look on Mom's face when Dad arrived home one day not long after the taxes were paid with a piano in the back of his wagon. Mom just couldn't believe her eyes, and after their neighbour, Calvin Stuart, helped Dad to move it from the wagon into the parlour she sat down, face beaming, and started to play. Right on cue, Dad pulled his violin out from under the sofa and started to play with her. She'd taken her guitar out of its case and throughout the night the three of them played nearly every song they knew for an appreciative family. What a joyful sound! How she wished for that close bond of making music together again. Since she'd been here she hadn't had time to practice playing her guitar hardly at all, with all of the work and homework she had to do. Not that she wasn't grateful for the opportunity to go to school, the things that she was learning were so exciting that she studied hard, continuing her high level of academic achievement.

Grandpa would be proud of me thought Ellen. He always said that I should continue at school, then go out and see the world.

Ellen's attention was caught by the sound of a horse and wagon pulling up close to their house below. She looked out of her window at the street that travelled towards the rows of houses and buildings in the town. When she unlatched the metal hook and opened the wood framed window to have a better look, the smell of steaming damp earth mixed with the farm smells and spilled into her room. The streets were still sleepy and except for an occasional dog barking they seemed deserted in the early Sunday light.

She returned to her comfortable chair and played with the worn down cording on the cushion of the soft deep armchair and her thoughts continued. She remembered Dad getting dressed up like an Indian for the Halloween dance at their community hall. He looked authentic in the costume Mom made for him, with fringes on the sleeves and pants, and on his head he wore a chief's headdress with feathers and long beads around his neck. He knew how to do the dances that the Indians did and performed them to perfection for the guests at the dance. Everyone loved it, including Dad, who whooped and chanted in time to the music. What a night that was!

Ellen's eyes started to droop and she relaxed into the warmth of the quilt wrapped around her in the wide armchair.

Hot tea always makes me drowsy Ellen thought as she opened her heavy eyes, then shut them again. It was so peaceful and quiet that she drifted away, her thoughts dormant, just below the surface of consciousness.

Off in the distance she could hear voices and the door shutting, then the sound of boots heavy on the stairs, plodding upstairs towards her room. Somewhere, far away, she thought that she could hear William's voice. It had to be a dream, and she drifted off again only to be startled awake by the heavy knock on her bedroom door.

Ellen shook herself awake and rose to answer the urgent thumping on her door. Still in a fog, Ellen opened her bedroom door and blinked at the tall figure standing in the shaded hallway.

"William! I thought I could hear you. Oh, it's so good to see you."

Ellen threw her arms around him in a warm embrace and, smiling, William hugged her back. He towered over Ellen now, slim, but with the muscular build of a young man and a face that had matured from a soft boyish look to the more angular features of a young adult. His dark wavy hair that had changed from the sandy blonde colour of his childhood shone in the early morning light that beamed in the hallway.

"Oh, I was just thinking about home. How are you? What brings you here on a Sunday morning? Never mind, you're here. Come in. Take your coat off."

William followed her in but he didn't take his coat off.

"You must be hungry or thirsty at least. Can I get you a cup of tea?"

"I'd like that Ellie. I guess I am a bit tired and thirsty."

"Tell me about home. How is everyone? Wait a minute. I'll be right back with some tea and maybe some toast to go with it. You can tell me all about home when I get back. Here, sit down and make yourself comfortable."

Without answering, William obediently found a chair and sat down, the smile fading from his face as he thought about the reason for his swift journey to see Ellen. He hadn't stopped to either eat or rest.

When Ellen returned she handed him a steaming cup of tea and a plate of toast. She hesitated, noting the serious look on her brother's face.

"Something is wrong, isn't it? William, what's wrong?"

"Everyone is okay, but Ellie, Dad needs you. I'm helping as much as I can but he needs all of our help."

"Why! What's wrong?"

"It's the horses. They've got sleeping sickness. Dad is devastated. We're trying to nurse them back to health, but it's difficult."

"Nell! Oh, no. Is my Nell sick?"

"So far Nell is okay, but the disease is going through some of the other horses. Ellie, can you come home and help us with them? We're doing everything we can, but it's too much. Dad is heartbroken. So many horses in our area have already died."

"Died!" Ellen exclaimed. Then, more softly to herself, she moaned, "That can't be. Died?"

"I'm sorry, Ellie but if you come with me now maybe you can help us with looking after the horses. We might be able to save them. I've already told the Schulzes and they'll deliver the milk themselves until you get back. Can you come with me now, Ellie?"

"Of course, William. Of course I will. Oh, Nell, please don't get sick."

Ellen nervously slipped into her coat that was still warm from her early morning milk delivery and in an alarmed panic searched for a few necessities to take with her.

She and William were soon making their way home to their farm. The miles slipped by, swallowed up with conversation about home and how they were dealing with the disease that was spreading amongst the horses.

"How did the horses get sick?" asked Ellen.

"You know that warm spell we've just had? Well, I guess the first batch of mosquitoes hatched, and they've spread the virus that causes the sleeping sickness in horses all around our area. Calvin Stuart stopped by and he said that the disease is everywhere. The first ones to get sick at our farm were the two young mares that Dad bought this year. We've all been working around the clock nursing them. So far, Nell and Sal here, are doing okay," said William, nodding at Sal who was pulling their wagon towards home.

"I didn't know that Dad bought some new horses this year."

"Yeah, one is a Morgan and the other one is a Quarter Horse that he got at an auction just three months ago. They're both pretty sick."

"Has the veterinarian seen them?"

"Dr. Williams was out two days ago. He called it enceph.... Uhh encephalomyelitis. Boy, that's a mouthful, but it's transmitted by infected mosquitoes. Lots of horses in our neighbourhood have already died from it. Ellie, you should see how awful it is when they get sick. They just get hot and sweaty and circle around aimlessly. They don't seem to know what they're doing. They don't eat or drink, they just shiver and pant with fever."

"Isn't there anything that can be done? Is there any medicine or anything for them?"

"No, Dr. Williams says that they need to be fed water in a bottle because they dehydrate very quickly. They just need to be made comfortable with cooling baths and to treat the fever as best we can."

The farmhouse looked the same when they pulled up beside their barn. Ellen climbed down from the wagon and looking up she saw Mom coming towards them. Her walk was slower than usual but when she got close to Ellen, she grabbed her in a warm and grateful hug, then hugged her again. Ellen was startled to see her Mom looking so haggard and tired. The stresses of caring for the sick animals was evident in her faded blue eyes.

"Where's Dad?" asked Ellen.

"I think he's still in the barn," said Mom.

"Come in for a moment and we'll talk," and arm in arm Mom and Ellen walked back to the house.

"Ellen!" came a feminine voice from the kitchen. "I'm so glad you're home."

Daisy put down the bowl that she was using to mix dough on the table and wiped her hands on a towel then moved to greet her sister.

"Daisy! Oh, Daisy," said Ellen and she hugged her in a large and happy embrace.

Even though her sister was still small for her age, she had grown as tall as Ellen's shoulders. Her thick curly dark hair was held back with a wide red ribbon that matched her red shirt and denim pants under the white apron she was wearing.

"Let me look at you. You're growing up. You look so beautiful, just like a young lady," Ellen said to a smiling Daisy.

"And who is this?" Ellen said to a wide eyed little face that was peering at her from behind Daisy. His blue eyes were squinted with the same frown that belonged to Mom and under one arm he was carrying Molly. He quickly retreated to safety further behind his sister, Daisy.

"I bet your name is Tommy," Ellen said.

Tommy continued to hide behind his sister until Daisy turned around and picked him up to face Ellen. Tommy was tall for his age and was quite an armful for Daisy when she picked him up. His small bare feet dangled from his blue denim bibbed overalls that covered a white t-shirt.

Silently, Mom pulled a kitchen chair away from the table to sit down on, then she pulled another one out for Ellen.

"Come and sit down, Ellen and I'll tell you what's been happening here."

"William told me that the horses had sleeping sickness and that a lot of horses in our area had already died."

"Our young mare, the Morgan, died this morning. The other one slipped into a coma just before you arrived. I don't expect she'll live through the day."

"Oh, Mom. I'm so sorry."

"That's not all. One of the dark Belgians is sick with the fever. She doesn't seem to know where she is. The sight of those horses in the field..."

Mom just shook her head as if she couldn't believe it.

"They just circle around until they can't anymore, then they just lay down and can't get up again. It's a terrible thing to see."

"Is Dad with them?"

"I believe so. He's been working through the night trying to get them to drink and eat, but so far nothing seems to be working."

"I think I should go and see what I can do to help," said Ellen rising from her chair. She looked at her mom's tired face and sagging shoulders and gave her hand a squeeze, then turned and headed out to the barn to see Dad.

Worried about what she would see in the barn, Ellen walked with a nervous trembling in her legs. She shivered, fearful, even though it wasn't cold outside, and her mind tossed about like a fluttering butterfly that didn't light on anything in particular, refusing to focus on what might lie ahead. She wasn't prepared and the greyness that swallowed her denied what she saw when she entered the barn.

She took small steps, apprehensive, inside through the wide open doorway of the barn that had always been so full of life with animal noises and smells. The shadows that were always friendly and full of subtle colours were heavy, dark and foreboding. There was a stench, a putrid odour, that overtook the smell of sweet hay and animal waste. Except for the soft sounds of quiet sobbing, the barn carried only a deathly stillness.

"Dad?" she almost whispered as she entered.

There was no answer and Ellen gingerly continued her search in the barn. In the first stall was their beautiful dark Belgian horse laying very still. Her blank dark eyes were robbed of intelligence and there was no breath left in her stiffening body. Only the circling black flies were in motion. Ellen looked away. The image that would be imprinted in her mind left a queasy feeling in her stomach.

She stopped and listened, then quietly walked to the next stall where she could see the outline of the back of her dad's shoulders shaking. Ellen stopped for a moment when she realized that her dad was crying. She'd never seen her dad cry before. He was always so happy and carefree. Nothing ever seemed to bother him. He was sitting in the hay with the Quarter Horse's head in his lap.

Ellen reached down and put her hand on his shoulder and he placed his other hand on top of hers.

"I'm home, Dad. I'm here to help."

Dad was still overcome with tears until he finally sighed and just patted her hand. He pulled himself up, leaving the horse's lifeless head to drop onto the hay. With one arm around her shoulders he guided

Ellen out of the barn and when they were in the open air he said,

"That's three of our horses we've lost. The Morgan is in the back field. Ellen, we need Nell to help us remove the Belgian and the Quarter Horse out to the same field as well."

"They're both gone then, Dad?"

"Our Belgian just died this morning. She went quick. She only showed symptoms yesterday. I hoped that I could nurse her but she collapsed into a coma once she was in the barn. Dr. Williams said they last about 2 to 3 days, but I guess it was just too much for her."

In the sunlight, Ellen could see her dad more clearly. He looked withered, and worn. The lines in his face, earned from hours of working outdoors in the sun, were deepened and it felt to Ellen that her dad had somehow weakened, had become smaller in stature and more vulnerable.

"What can I do, Dad?" said Ellen.

"We need to get Nell out of the pasture," said Dad in a small and breaking voice. "Can you bring her to the barn, Ellen?"

"What do you want Nell to do?"

Dad looked away, and without answering Ellen's question he said, "If you bring her to the barn door it would be a big help. I need to check to see how William is doing."

After taking the lead halter off of the hook on the beam in the barn, Ellen followed the path to the pasture that was east of the house and barn. She silently prayed all the way that she would find Nell happy and energetic. She hoped for a miracle that Nell would be spared from this dreadful disease, a dark curtain of death, that was claiming the lives of their horses.

"Nell, oh Nell!" Ellen cried when she saw Nell standing in the field. Ellen whistled again, then called, "Nell. Come on, girl. It's me, Nell. Come on."

Nell looked at her in disbelief but when she recognized that it was Ellen, Nell started with a jerk, then trotted towards Ellen. She held out her hand and reached to stroke Nell. Ellen was so relieved to see her that she laid her head against Nell's neck and stroked her velvety coat. Nell made soft loving and welcoming gestures and whinnies.

"Looks like we've got another job to do, you and I," whispered Ellen. "You'll have to come with me, Nell. Dad needs our help."

Nell looked at her and nodded understanding while Ellen slipped the lead halter over her head and started to lead her back towards the barn.

Dad threw a heavy harness over Nell's back and tightened and buckled it up and then opened the door of the stall where the dead Belgian horse was laying. Then he hitched it to a harness that he'd wrapped around the motionless belly of the Belgian horse. Nell's eyes were wide and bulging with fear, her nose lifting as though she wanted to extinguish the awful smell of death that was all around her. She knew what her dreadful task was and the terror was reflected in her dark eyes.

"Maybe you should hitch up Sal with Nell. That's a pretty heavy load for her," Ellen said.

Dad looked at Ellen and weakly explained that Sal was starting to act a bit funny.

"But she was fine on the ride home," said Ellen.

"I know, but she seems like she's developing a fever," said Dad.

Ellen was stunned, wordless, as Dad continued on with his dismal job. He took the lead reins and urged Nell on,

"Come on, girl. Let's go. Come on now."

Nell strained at the heavy load, pulling with all of her might and with a great effort she managed to start moving the Belgian horse from its resting spot. Slowly, the Belgian slid out, and with Nell pulling her, they made their way towards the opening of the barn, out of the dark tomb and into the daylight. That terrible load was pulled all the way to the back field, where William was busy digging graves for the dead horses in the soft grassy field.

The sound of his shovel hitting the earth was their funeral dirge, and the requiem mass was held by the circling turkey buzzards high in the sky above them.

Ellen watched as Nell pulled the two dead horses to the back field. Like a searing branding iron that scorches a tender young hide, the sight of the dead horses laying in the field burned and melted into her memory.

"I'm going to help William," said Dad. "Will you take a look at Sal and the other Belgian. They'll need some care. They need to be fed fluids from a bottle."

"Where are they?" asked Ellen.

"Over in that pasture over there," answered Dad pointing in their direction.

Trembling, Ellen walked to the gate that contained the pasture on the west side of the house. Her heart nearly stopped when she saw their once strong Belgian sitting in the grass and pressing its head into the ground. Ellen coaxed her onto her feet and led her back to the barn. Throughout the rest of the day and into the night Ellen helped Dad, Mom and William wash her down with an alcohol rub and feed her liquids from a bottle. Eventually Sal joined the Belgian in the barn where she too had to be cared for with rub downs and forced liquids to help ward off the fever.

By daybreak, their Belgian had succumbed to the sleeping sickness and she too lay still, spiritless and silent. Nell, still strong, pulled her to the burial site in the back field.

In spite of their exhaustion, the family continued to try to help their afflicted horse, Sal. It was no use. Sal's fever and her advancing age worked against her and she died the following morning, two days after Ellen arrived home.

Ellen now felt as exhausted as her mom and dad looked. She found her way into the house for a rest, dropped into her old bed, felt the warmth of the homemade quilts that had kept her warm for as long as she could remember, and closed her tired sore eyes.

Please keep Nell safe she pleaded into the still air before drifting off to sleep.

She awoke to the aroma of dinner cooking, sniffed, then breathed it in. The events of the past two days were still lost in her fuzzy sleep.

"Stew," she thought. "It smells like Mom has made stew. I hope she has some homemade bread to go with it."

Slowly the memory of the past two days returned. The dark cave that her thoughts inhabited closed in with no visible way out.

"Nell," she wondered out loud. "Is Nell still all right?"

Ellen went downstairs where her subdued family was just sitting down to dinner. Tommy was picking the peas out of his bowl of stew and happily dropping them on the floor. He looked at his mom and dad but nobody was watching him so he continued with his play of dive bombing with the green peas splashing around the legs of his chair.

"You have to eat something, Billy," said Mom. "And you too, William."

"I wish I was hungry," said Dad.

"You've been up for several nights with very little rest. I don't want you to get sick too."

Dad played with his stew, then put his spoon down and rested his head in his hand, elbow on the table, as if his head was just too heavy for him to carry anymore.

"I fell asleep. Is Nell still all right?" said Ellen.

"So far she's okay," said Dad. "Let's hope that she won't get it."

Ellen, a steaming bowl of stew in her hand, sat down beside William and quietly ate her dinner. She was at least grateful that Nell wasn't sick.

Ellen slept fitfully that night, awakening early the next morning when she thought she could hear Dad downstairs, and carefully slipped out of bed not wanting to wake Daisy. She found Dad in the kitchen. He looked tired as if he hadn't slept much at all again last night.

Ellen started to ask Dad if things were all right but she stopped when he looked at her and brokenly said,

"I'm sorry, Ellen."

Before the words were out of his mouth, Ellen knew what he was about to say.

"No." she wailed. "It can't be."

"Nell is in the barn now. She's got the fever. All we can do is try to save her, but she's looking pretty sick."

Ellen rushed out to the barn ignoring the early morning coolness. Nell was there in her stall, where she lay shivering but immobilized by the great feverishness that had overtaken her. Her eyes were dull looking, as though they wanted to withdraw in confusion, and she wouldn't either eat or drink.

"Oh, Nell. Why did you have to get sick too?"

There was no answer to her question. Only the cold and awful silence in the darkness that was haloed by the breaking dawn.

Ellen felt her dad's arm around her shoulder. She collapsed in tears, head bowed into her dad.

"Don't give up, Ellen. Don't ever give up.

Some horses have survived this terrible disease."

"Oh, Dad. Why did this have to happen?"

"I don't know, Ellen. I just don't know. Come on. You need to get dressed and have something to eat. I'll stay here with Nell until you get back. Bring a fresh bottle to feed her with and some rubbing alcohol and fresh damp rags to cool her down with."

Throughout the day, Ellen stayed with Nell. She stroked her neck and talked to her while wiping away the sweat on her body and feeding her water from the glass bottle that Mom gave her. At first, Nell refused to drink, and the water ran down her chin and dribbled onto the hay that they were resting on. Except for the short rapid pants and shivering, she was immobile, lying on her side in the hay in her stall, vacant and disinterested in the cool water that Ellen was trying to get her to drink.

"Come on, girl. You have to drink," whispered Ellen into Nell's ear.

Eventually, with persistence, Ellen was able to coax Nell into swallowing some of the cooling water. The sound of Ellen's voice seemed to bring back a small flicker of light in Nell's eyes and Ellen wasn't sure but she thought that she still recognized her. She hadn't yet slipped away into that deep dark pit of unconscious confusion.

Nell's panting came slower and more shallow as the day began to turn into evening but Ellen kept talking to her: "You know, Nell, the first time I saw you I thought that you were the most beautiful creature I'd ever seen. How I loved to ride you. You were so proud and energetic. And all these years you've been my best friend. You were always there for me.

Didn't you just love the songs I sang to you, our talks about just about everything and the fast rides to the post office? Oh, those rides, galloping with the wind in our faces. We didn't have a care in the world, Nell. We were free to run with nothing but our dreams and an open road ahead. Remember the first snowfall, the wild flowers in the fields in spring and the picnics in the warm sun in the summertime? You've got to get better, Nell."

Ellen's voice caught and two salty tears bubbled up in her tired eyes then slid down her cheeks as she stroked Nell's feverish neck.

"We love you, Nell. Please don't die," Ellen choked.

A long shadow formed from behind Ellen just as the sparkling gold and orange evening sun was about to set. It cast a glow on the edges of the doorway of the barn and lit up and haloed her mom who was now standing behind her. Mom silently wiped the tears from her eyes, then put her hand on Ellen's shoulder and gave her a knowing pat.

"Would you like me to sit with her for a while? You could use a rest."

"No, Mom. I'm fine. I'm going to stay for as long as Nell needs me."

The setting sun glowed, lighting up the world in a final farewell to the day, then disappeared behind the distant hills, and the landscape slowly turned from a fuzzy grey to quiet darkness. While the moon rose in the sky they both slept with Ellen curled up in the stall with her arm wrapped around Nell's neck and her head nestled against her hot body.

Ellen stirred in the rustling hay. Without thinking, she pulled up the thin blanket that had been carefully placed on her last night. The sun was rising on the horizon creating a new pink and blue dawn in a brand new day. She opened her eyes, then closed them again until she felt a warm nuzzle nudging against her cheek. Ellen started to drift off to sleep again until memory suddenly returned and she opened her eyes wide. It was Nell. She was touching and sniffing her. Ellen realized that Nell was no longer over heated. The fever was gone and Nell was looking at her with eyes that recognized and loved her.

"Nell! Are you really okay?"

Nell gave her a weary small nod and a soft whinny then put her head down for more rest. Ellen could hardly contain her excitement. She hugged Nell and patted her.

"Good girl, Nell. I knew you could do it."

Her dad appeared from out of the early morning shadows. It was the first smile he'd worn since the horses first became ill with the deadly virus.

Nell was very tired for her first few days of convalescing but eventually she was able to function normally. She never recovered her full energy though. It was as if the sleeping sickness had sucked some of the life out of her. Ellen stayed at home on the farm to look after Nell until she had to return to the Schultz' dairy farm and finish her term at school.

On the day that she was to leave in the wagon drawn by a donkey that Dad bought, she said goodbye to Nell, then hugged her mom, Tommy and Daisy. When it was Dad's turn he looked away embarrassed by the tears that were welling in his eyes. You see, Dad didn't like goodbyes and especially today he found it impossible to say farewell to his oldest daughter as she was leaving home once more.

As the wagon pulled away with Ellen and William in it, Ellen looked back at their farm, her mom, Daisy, Tommy and her dad, then at the sky above. The wind that was blowing through the waving grassy fields below and the grey and white cumulous clouds above murmured in Ellen's ears that life was constantly changing, but in spite of its unpredictability the love and memories she shared with her family growing up remained constant. They were memories that she would always cherish and carry with her no matter where she went.

She looked ahead again with courage and resolve.

Life is like the clouds she thought, always changing as they dance in the wind that flies across a prairie sky.

Author's Note

The ravages of the western equine viral encephomyelitis that plagued the western prairies in Canada and parts of the United States during the 1930's has been held in check by a vaccine which given to horses together with other vaccinations administered in early May offers protection from the deadly virus.

About the Author

Karen Poirier was born in Vancouver, British Columbia. She moved to Port Alberni in 1967 and now resides there with her husband. Her home and studio can be found on acreage in the outskirts of the city. The studio where she paints and writes overlooks a beautiful and extensive flower and vegetable garden and is appropriately named Country Roads Studio. After a lifetime of involvement in two dimensional art with many awards in Juried exhibitions, group and solo shows, Karen discovered an interest in writing. You can visit her on facebook.

CPSIA information can be obtained at www.ICGtesting.com
Printed in the USA
LVOW07s0741300814

401544LV00001B/8/P